Critical Praise for
THE SUN, THE MOON, AND THE STARS

"AN EXCITING EXAMPLE OF HOW FANTASY MAY BE COMBINED WITH MODERN THEMES AND PERCEPTIONS . . . The search for artistic and personal balance and riches, the battle of a lifetime, and the poignant portrait of an artist out of touch with the everyday world are themes Brust presents with flair and style . . . with dark and unpredictable twists and turns of plot and interactions between fantasy and reality which keep the reader engrossed to the end."
— *Midwest Book Review*

"Brust stretches the boundaries of our field . . . stirs some unexpected emotions." — *Denver Post*

"Highly experimental . . . It's my kind of book!"
— *Locus*

"Brust uses the mirror of folklore as commentary and reflection on his characters' real world obstacles to success. Recommended!" — *Library Journal*

STEVEN BRUST

Steven Brust is the author of six popular and critically acclaimed books: *Brokedown Palace*, *To Reign in Hell*, and the books of the Vlad Taltos series, which includes *Jhereg*, *Yendi*, *Teckla*, and *Taltos*. He is a founding member of the legendary Minneapolis Scribblies Fantasy Writers' Group, and has a fierce appreciation for all things Hungarian.

THE SUN THE MOON AND THE STARS

STEVEN BRUST

ARMADILLO PRESS
INCORPORATED
NEW YORK·NEW YORK

ACE BOOKS, NEW YORK

The Fairy Tales series is produced by
Armadillo Press, Inc., 648 Broadway, Suite 700,
New York, NY 10012.

This Ace book contains the complete
text of the original hardcover edition.

THE SUN, THE MOON, AND THE STARS

An Ace Book / published by arrangement with
Armadillo Press, Inc.

PRINTING HISTORY
Ace Hardcover edition / May 1987
Ace edition / October 1988

ISBN: 0-441-79099-2

10 9 8 7 6 5 4 3 2 1

◆ FOR TERRI ◆

My thanks to:

Erin McKee, Ken Fletcher, Michael
Butler, Martin Schafer, Rich Adamaski,
Terri Windling, Thomas Canty,
Bill Brust, Nate Bucklin, Emma Bull,
Kara Dalkey, Pamela Dean, Will
Shetterly, and Matthew B. Tepper
for help on this project.

◆

And special thanks to my son,
Corwin, for baby-sitting above and
beyond the call . . .

◆

Steven Brust, October 1986
Minneapolis, Minnesota

INTRODUCTION
•FAIRY TALES•

There is no satisfactory equivalent to the German word *märchen*, tales of magic and wonder such as those collected by the Brothers Grimm: *Rapunzel, Hansel & Gretel, Rumpelstiltskin, The Six Swans* and other such familiar stories. We call them fairy tales, although none of the above stories actually contains a creature called a "fairy". They do contain those ingredients most familiar to us in fairy tales: magic and enchantment, spells and curses, witches and trolls, and protagonists who defeat overwhelming odds to triumph over evil. J.R.R. Tolkien, in his classic essay on Fairy Stories, offers the definition that these are not in particular tales about fairies or elves, but rather of the land of Faerie: "the Perilous Realm itself, and the air that blows in the country. I will not attempt to define that directly," he goes on, "for it cannot be done. Faerie cannot be caught in a net of words; for it is one of its qualities to be indescribable, though not imperceptible."

Fairy tales were originally created for an adult audience. The tales collected in the German countryside and set to paper by the Brothers Grimm (wherein a Queen orders her step-daughter, Snow White, killed and her heart served "boiled and salted for my dinner" and a peasant girl must cut off her own feet lest the Red Shoes, of which she has been so vain, keep her dancing night and day until she dances herself to death) were published for an adult readership, popular, in the age of Göethe and Schiller, among the German Romantic poets. Charles Perrault's spare and moralistic tales (such as Little Red Riding Hood who, in the original Perrault telling, gets eaten by the wolf in the end for having the ill sense to talk to strangers in the wood) was written for the court of Louis XIV; Madame d'Aulnoy (author of *The White Cat)* and Madame Leprince de Beaumont (author of *Beauty and the Beast)* also wrote for the French aristocracy. In England, fairy stories and heroic legends were popularized through Mallory's Arthur, Shakespeare's Puck and Ariel, Spenser's Faerie Queene.

With the Age of Enlightenment and the growing emphasis on rational and scientific modes of thought, along with the rise in fashion of novels of social realism in the Nineteenth Century, literary fantasy went out of vogue and those stories of magic, enchantment, heroic quests and courtly romance that form a cultural heritage thousands of years old, dating back to the oldest written epics and further still to tales spoken around the hearthfire, came to be seen as fit only for children, relegated to the nursery like, Professor Tolkien points out, "shabby or old fashioned furniture . . . primarily because the adults do not want it, and do not mind if it is misused."

And misused the stories have been, in some cases altered so greatly to make them suitable for Victorian children that the original tales were all but forgotten. Andrew Lang's *Tam Lin*, printed in the colored Fairy Books series, tells the story of little Janet whose playmate is stolen away by the fairy folk—ignoring the original, darker tale of seduction and human sacrifice to the Lord of Hell, as the heroine, pregnant with Tam Lin's child, battles the Fairy Queen for her lover's life. Walt Disney's "Sleeping Beauty" bears only a little resemblance to Straparola's *Sleeping Beauty of the Wood*, published in Venice in the Sixteenth Century, in which the enchanted princess is impregnated as she sleeps. The Little Golden Book version of the *Arabian Nights* resembles not at all the violent and sensual tales recounted by Scheherzade in *One Thousand and One Nights* so that the King of Kings won't take her virginity and her life.

The wealth of material from myth and folklore at the disposal of the story-teller (or modern fantasy novelist) has been described as a giant cauldron of soup into which each generation throws new bits of fancy and history, new imaginings, new ideas, to simmer along with the old. The story-teller is the cook who serves up the common ingredients in his or her own individual way, to suit the tastes of a new audience. Each generation has its cooks, its Hans Christian Andersen or Charles Perrault, spinning magical tales for those who will listen—even amid the Industrial Revolution of the Nineteenth Century or the technological revolution of our own. In the last century, George MacDonald, William Morris, Christina Rossetti, and Oscar Wilde, among others, turned their hands to fairy stories; at the turn of the century lavish fairy tale collections were produced, a showcase for the art of Arthur Rackham, Edmund Dulac, Kay Nielson, the Robinson Brothers—published as children's books, yet often found gracing adult salons.

In the early part of the Twentieth Century Lord Dunsany, G.K. Chesterton, C.S. Lewis, T.H. White, J.R.R. Tolkien—to name but a few—created classic tales of fantasy; while more recently we've seen the growing popularity of books published under the category title "Adult Fantasy"—as well as works published in the literary mainstream that could easily go under that heading: John Barth's *Chimera*, John Gardner's *Grendel*, Joyce Carol Oates' *Bellefleur*, Sylvia Townsend Warner's *Kingdoms of Elfin*, Mark Halprin's *A Winter's Tale*, and the works of South American writers such as Gabriel García Márquez and Miguel Angè Asturias.

It is not surprising that modern readers or writers should occasionally turn to fairy tales. The fantasy story or novel differs from novels of social realism in that it is free to portray the world in bright, primary colors, a dream-world half remembered from the stories of childhood when all the world was bright and strange, a fiction unembarrassed to tackle the large themes of Good and Evil, Honor and Betrayal, Love and Hate. Susan Cooper, who won the Newbery Medal for her fantasy novel *The Grey King*, makes this comment about the desire to write fantasy: "In the 'Poetics' Aristotle said, 'A likely impossibility is always preferable to an unconvincing possibility.' I think those of us who write fantasy are dedicated to making impossible things seem likely, making dreams seem real. We are somewhere between the Impressionist and abstract painters. Our writing is haunted by those parts of our experience which we do not understand, or even consciously remember. And if you, child or adult, are drawn to our work, your response comes from that same shadowy land."

All Adult Fantasy stories draw in a greater or lesser degree from traditional tales and legends. Some writers consciously acknowledge that material, such as J.R.R. Tolkien's use of themes and imagery from the Icelandic Eddas and the German Niebelungenlied in *The Lord of the Rings* or Evangeline Walton's reworking of the stories from the Welsh Mabinogion in *The Island of the Mighty*. Some authors use the language and symbols of old tales to create new ones, such as the stories collected in Jane Yolen's *Tales of Wonder*, or Patricia McKillip's *The Forgotten Beasts of Eld*. And others, like Robin McKinley in *Beauty* or Angela Carter in *The Bloody Chamber* (and the movie "The Company of Wolves" derived from a story in that collection) base their stories directly on old tales, breathing new life into them, and presenting them to the modern reader.

The Fairy Tales series, created by Armadillo Press and published by Ace Fantasy Books, presents new novels of the later sort—novels directly based on traditional fairy tales. Each novel in the series is firmly based on a specific, often familiar, tale—yet each author is free to use that tale as he or she pleases, showing the diverse ways a modern story-teller can approach traditional material.

The novel you hold in your hands, *The Sun, the Moon, and the Stars,* makes use of a Hungarian fairy tale to parallel and highlight a realistic story about an artist's struggle to create. Future Fairy Tales include a more straightforward fantasy retelling of Hans Christian Andersen's *The Nightingale,* a contemporary rendition of *Jack the Giant-killer* in which the Faery Court lurks in the shadows of modern-day Ottawa . . . and much more. Fantasy and horror by some of the most talented writers in these two fields, retelling the world's most beloved tales, in editions lovingly designed—as all good Fairy Tale books should be. We hope you'll enjoy them.

T. W.

THE SUN THE MOON AND THE STARS

CHAPTER
• ONE •

1. *THE LAMENTATION*

YOU WANT TO KNOW what good is? I'll tell
you what good is.

My freshman year at the University my roommate
was a guy named Phil. In addition to the room, we
shared a couple of art classes and a weakness for Girodet.
We were in one of the newer dorms, all shiny and tiny
and boring and beige. One time when we were bitching
about how cramped it was, he got a funny look in his
eyes. I hardly saw him for the next week. Then, when I

came in one evening, I almost choked on the apple I was eating. I stood there, half in and half out of the room, trying to simultaneously stare at what Phil had done while gasping and coughing around the piece of apple. I'm sure it was quite comical, but I was too busy to notice whether Phil was laughing at me.

He'd done this painting, you see. An oil. The edges of it exactly matched the edges of the far wall of the room, right down to half the smudge where Phil's girlfriend had thrown a beer at me (that's another story). The painting covered over the window, and you'd swear there was another room there. It was perfect. The doorway was a dark hardwood, with knots in it here and there, and textbooks were off to one side in their own bookcase; he'd given me a huge wooden desk, while I could see half of a glass desk for Phil, and there were these big speakers, and I could see the label on the SONY amplifier.

It was when I found myself grimacing with annoyance at the color of the carpet on Phil's side of the room and being glad it wasn't under my chair that it really hit me.

Do you have any idea of what must have gone into that? It isn't just the perfection of the illusion; he also had to know me well enough to create a room that was mine and his—that is, that reflected both of our personalities, as well as the sorts of compromises we'd reach if we'd had another room and enough money to furnish it. He had my half just a bit messier than his, and in just the right ways—including scattered albums of some people I'm sure I hadn't told him I liked.

The thing was up for the rest of the year, and I never got tired of looking at it. It was scary that he knew me that well, but that didn't hit me until later.

Right then I gave him the kind of reaction he must have wanted—oohing and ahhing and pointing out details. I'm sure he was satisfied, and I didn't have to fake my reaction at all. I hung around a little longer, then I went off into the corner room of the dorm where the floor's refrigerator lived, and I locked the door, and I cried, because I knew I'd never be able to do something like that.

That's what good is.

I ran into Phil a couple of years ago. He's now doing billboards—excuse me—Outdoor Advertising.

What can you say?

2. *The Annunciation*

It's too much to hope for that everything I paint will be better than what I did before, but I can try. I used to think that once I'd mastered composition, and perspective, and form, I could forget about them and just think about art. I don't think so anymore.

Maybe some people can do that, but for me, it's like karate: the more I learn, the more I have to concentrate on simple technique. For instance, Sensei yelled at me the other day about hip rotation. Hip rotation, for God's sake. I should have mastered that when I was sixth kyu, and now I'm getting ready to test for shodan and I have to work on my bleeding hips.

Maybe it's a basic flaw in my personality, but it's just the same with painting. The more I try to accomplish, the more I have to work on the basics. Is it like that for everyone? I doubt it. I should probably study some art history; it might make me feel better. But do you have any idea how boring art history is? Karen is the expert of the five of us, and, well, I have to admit her painting doesn't impress me as much as, say, Dan's. But that isn't fair; Dan is a genius.

I used to wish I was a genius. I guess maybe I still do. But then, that old cliché about challenging yourself is true; there's a certain satisfaction that comes from pushing your limits. Of course, sometimes you fall flat on your face. But you have to try, don't you?

3. *The Marriage of St. Francis to Poverty*

Robert came bounding into the studio wearing biker leathers and studs and an honest-to-god French beret. He's short and anemic looking, with big, hollow brown eyes and dark hair that he has restyled about every half hour. Right then it was fairly long and pushed back behind the beret.

I said, "Where'dya find that, Unca Bobby?"

He nodded a laidback hello and said, "Rag stock. Would you believe two dollars?"

"Yeah? They have any more?"

He shook his head. "How was training?"

"Great," I lied. "You should join. Then you can be really tough."

"Yeah. Like you. I will, one of these days. Let's grab everyone and do some dancing tonight." He chacha'd in place to emphasize the point.

I gave an exaggerated look around the place. The studio is long, with two huge windows flanking the door, both of which are presently covered by thick black drapes. At the opposite end is a balcony, or really a deck, about eight feet above the floor, reached by an iron stairway. Robert's area is back and to the left as you face it, Dan has the front right. Dan works with his back to the rest of us, so whatever he's working on is usually the second thing you notice when you walk in, even before the wall decorations hit your eye. The first thing you'll respond to though, is the ceiling, even if you aren't aware of it. It's high, with exposed rafters below a steep roof. When you walk in the door, your eye automatically travels up to it, lifting you, raising your spirits. We're all agreed that that was what sold us on the place, although none of us were aware of it at the time. The walls are our joint project;

even Dan gets willy when he works on them. They're full of garish blues and yellows and swaths of red two feet thick, in a style Karen calls, "Post-Urban Subway."

Anyway, I gave a look around the studio and said, "Everyone doesn't seem to be around, Unca Bobby."

"So call 'em, bozo."

"No, I want to get some work done."

"You? Work?"

"You can shut up now."

"Yes, sir." He looked around my area. "You ever going to clean up this dump, or what?"

"Eat raw fish and die, white boy."

"Guess not, huh? So what's cooking?"

Actually I hadn't decided, except that I was ready to start on something. Just for the hell of it, I said, "I'm thinking about hauling out the big one."

He turned serious. "Are you really? The Monster?"

I nodded, wondering if I was actually going to. A year before then, I'd made my first (and, to date, only) sale of more than a hundred bucks, and to celebrate I'd bought and sized this six by nine canvas, like they used in art school and nobody ever wants to buy. Dan had just given me a lecture about painting bigger, and when he saw it, he nodded and went back to working on another masterpiece that wouldn't sell. The Monster had been sitting in the back room since then.

Robert whistled, then said, "Arnold says the rent is due." He was referring to the fifth member of our little band, David, who goes through occasional stretches of body building. (Get it? Body building? Stretches? Never mind.) Robert calls him Arnold Schwarzenegger when he isn't around.

I ignored the comment about the rent because it would just frustrate me. I truly loathe and despise money and all things associated with it, and I will continue to do so until I'm making enough so I don't have to worry about it.

He decided not to let it die. "We need to come up with some cash, chum."

I said, "Yeah."

"Will your old lady—?"

"Don't call her that."

He isn't as much of an asshole as this makes him sound; he just knows how to make me mad, and does it whenever he thinks I'm tuning him out. One of these days I'm probably going to belt him for it. I've been sponging off Deb for two years, now, and I've never felt good about it, and Robert knows that. He's really not a bad guy; I don't know why he does things like that to me. Maybe if I hit him just once . . .

"All right, Debbie, then. Is she going to be able to—?"

"We're trying to come up with our own rent, Robert. We'll try to kick in what we can."

"You know, if we all got a big house together—"

"I know. I've heard it before. We'd kill each other inside of a month."

"How do you know that? It doesn't make sense for each of us to pay our own rent, and have to pay again for the studio."

I didn't answer, hoping to shut him up. It worked, this time. He leaned back against the wall near the door and watched me. I sighed to myself and went into the back room to get the Monster. I might as well set it up. Hell, I might as well try to paint something on it, though I had no idea what.

When I got back, Robert was staring at David's latest project, an oil portrait of the waitress at Bill and Toni's. I set the Monster down and said, "I like it. He had the whole background sketched in at first, remember?"

"Yeah. I like it this way, with the choppy effect instead, and nothing behind her."

I nodded. "Like she's formed from the color. It's nice."

I was pleased that he agreed, since I was the one who suggested to David that he lose the restaurant background and just concentrate on the figure.

Robert returned to my area and helped me argue with a pair of easels until they agreed to hold The Monster. I'd need to set the canvas on the floor to do the top third or my arm would fall off, but I could start this way.

"What's the project?" asked Robert, damn his eyes.

"I'm going back to the classics."

"The classics?"

"Yeah. Something Greek. You know, Zeus raping Athena, or whoever it was."

"Are you serious?"

"No."

"Good."

I stopped and looked at him, but decided not to pursue it.

He said, "So what *are* you going to do?"

I pulled on a few switches to turn some of the spot-lights on, then moved the stepladder over and played them until they were right. I didn't burn myself too badly. Experience, son. I went for a kind of natural morning light, for no reason that I can identify.

I moved the ladder out of the way, then picked up my palette and squeezed out some flake white onto four separate spots around it, then light chrome interspersed with it in three spots. I love flake white. It makes me want to lick my brushes. Sorry if that's too grotesque for you. "Paint," I said.

"No, but are you going to do something classical?"

I squeezed out the ochre yellow. I love squeezing paint onto the palette. It reminds me of fingerpainting. I'm always tempted to squeeze it onto my hands and work that way. Dan did that once, for part of a beach scene and it worked for him. I said, "Why not?"

"Too much research," said Robert.

I shrugged. "Depends what I want to do with it."

"I guess. Gonna sketch first?"

"No."

"Just diving right in, eh?"

"Yeah. What the hell? I'm feeling gutsy today."

"In that case, are you sure you don't want to go out to The Revue tonight?"

"Who's playing?"

"This is Friday? Bob Berlien and the White Women, I think."

"Forget it. I don't have that much energy. Maybe tomorrow."

"Okay."

He hung around for a few more minutes, then walked out, setting the stupid chimes tinkling and leaving me alone in the big studio, and a minute later I heard his Yamaha fire up. I noticed the silence that I hadn't been aware of before. After a moment, I was noticing traffic sounds coming from North Lincoln, a block away. I knew there would come a time when I'd want more noise than this to work to, but, for reasons I can't figure out, not when I'm starting. That's partly why I always try to start paintings on Friday or Saturday evening, when I often have the studio to myself.

I set the palette down on the table to my left, and started laying out brushes and stuff on my right. I pulled up the bar stool I always sit on when I work and that's going to be responsible for destroying my back some day. I stared back at the Monster. "I'm gonna getcha," I told it.

It didn't deign to answer.

4. *The Birth of the Virgin*

Robert and David say they are intimidated by empty canvas (or paper, in Robert's case). I feel a kind of exhilaration when I stare at it. I'm a bit frightened, too, but there is this incredible *potential* staring at me. I can go *anywhere* with it.

Sometimes I have an idea of what I'm after. In fact, most of the time I know almost exactly what I want it to look like; I'll do eight or nine sketches, then transfer it to the canvas. But just attacking the thing with the first color I come to and seeing what it is that takes shape is more fun. It's also more risky, but that's just another way of saying the same thing. I'll admit that I had doubts about trying that with a canvas this big, though. Dan had suggested that I go for a large effect, like they made us do at the "U", and that meant working hard on balancing the forms and everything. But, on the other hand, I thought about how much fun it would be to take on something this size just by feel and to have it work.

I've never been good at resisting temptation.

I stared at the canvas and my hand found the palette knife. I stared some more, and stepped back to try to grasp the whole size. It was bigger than anything I'd done before, even in school. I moved back and forth a bit, glanced at my palette, and drew in some ivory black, mixed it with viridian, white, and some ochre yellow. I studied the sort of green I'd produced and added a bit more white. The result was a very light green-gray that just hinted at some blue highlights. On the canvas it would be—how do I say it—*sensitive*. If I started with a background like that, I might have to make up for it later. I mean, there was nothing vibrant about it, and I'm not into making oils that look like pastels. But I liked it. It had character, you know what I mean?

I set down the palette knife and took up my favorite half-inch brush; hard bristles, unyielding, assertive.

I got the brush wet and attacked.

5. *The Meeting at the Golden Gate*

Once upon a time there were three Gypsies playing in a thicket near a road. One of them would gather up dust from the road, the second would build it into a mound, and the third would squash it flat. Then they would all roll on the ground, laughing in the fashion of Gypsies, their hands clasped together in front of their bellies.

Who knows how they came to be there? Perhaps their poor father, having no way to feed them, left them there. Perhaps they wandered off from their camp and became lost. It could even be that they were created there, out of the very dust with which they played. I don't know, but I know they were there, because I saw them myself, as I had pulled off the road to rest my horses and have a drink of *pálinka*.

In fact, I was going to offer them a drink, when a man dressed in a yellow gown came along the road and stopped before them. They looked at him, and he looked at them, and pretty soon up comes another man, dressed in a white gown, and stops next to the first and he looks at the Gypsies too. And pretty soon a third man comes along, and he has a black gown, and he stops by the first two. A fourth man comes along then, and he's dressed in green.

Well, just then the first one, who had the yellow gown, says to the second, "Brother, our master the King has commanded us to spread the word to all living souls, whomever or wherever we may find them, even if they are only three Gypsy boys living in the thicket by the side of the road."

The second man (he had the white gown, you remember) nodded and turned to the third man. "Well, brother, we should begin then with these three Gypsy boys, who are playing in the dust."

The third man, who was dressed in black, turned to the fourth man, and he said, "Our three hundred and sixty-two comrades will be along soon. We can get the jump on them if you will tell these three Gypsy boys of our quest, and then we can go on the next."

The fourth man (he was in green, if you recall) nodded and addressed the Gypsies, saying, "As you know, we do not now have a sun, a moon, or any stars." (I forgot to mention that this happened long ago, before we had the sun, the moon, or the stars.)

"Well, our master, who is King of all his Kingdom, will give half of this Kingdom and his daughter's hand in marriage to anyone who can fix the sun, the moon, and the stars in the heavens."

Well, two of the Gypsies started laughing, and the four men started to leave, but the youngest of the Gypsies stood up and he said, "Go no further. My name is Csucskári the Gypsy, and these are my brothers who are called Holló and Bagoly, and you may tell the King that between us we will do as he wishes." (You might say that Csucskári should have said *among* us, but he was young and a Gypsy, so don't judge him too harshly.) He went on, then, and said, "But, to do this, the King must bring us three things. First, he must bring us the tallest tree in the world, for we will need to climb very high to fix the sun, the moon, and the stars. Next, he must bring us a rope that will go all around the world, so we can stop the world to put the sun, the moon, and the stars in place. Third, he must bring us an iron skillet and two eggs so we can eat breakfast."

Well, the four counselors (for that's what they were) hurried off, and soon came back with the iron skillet and the eggs, and the three Gypsy boys sat down to breakfast. While they were eating, one of his brothers said, "Come now, Csucskári, you have earned us a meal for nothing, it is true, but surely you are having a joke with the foolish counselors, aren't you?"

Csucskári said, "No, Holló." (The one who had spoken was Holló.) "All we need are those things I have asked for and I will do as I have promised." Then he told them that he was a *taltos*, and, in fact, he hadn't eaten any breakfast, but had left the eggs for his brothers, for a *taltos* can't eat, as we all know. "You, my dear brothers, must agree to let me lead in all matters concerning this business, and I promise you that we will all become rich, and I will marry the King's daughter."

Well, his brothers agreed, and they settled down to wait for the King's counselors to return.

6. St. John the Baptist
Leaving the City for the Wilderness

Beginnings are difficult times. There's so much there. Potential, of course. And uncertainty, along with his older brother, fear. Excitement. Setting out blind is the worst, as well as the best.

When you work this way you're opening yourself up completely. You're working from your soul, and if those you respect (and, at least as important, those who don't know you from Adam) don't like it, there's no way around it: it's your soul they don't like.

So what do you have to fall back on? Technique. I've worked hard to build up technique, always hoping it would run itself, like a reverse punch follows an inside block. I've got it now, right at my fingertips, so to speak. All of my past, all of the things that surround my life and make me who I am and who I am becoming, the eye that I desperately hope can tell good from bad, the demons of imagination that buzz around my subconscious and direct the labor—all these are what I can count on.

Later I won't be thinking about this, I'll be thinking about what I'm doing, but at the beginning I can't help it; I step back, just as I will at the end, and hope for success as if it were something beyond my control.

I stand naked before you.

Bones?

CHAPTER ·TWO·

1. MARTIN VAN NIEUWENHOVE

DAVID AND I WERE sitting around the studio one day, shortly after we'd set the place up, swapping school stories. I mentioned how boring I'd found freshman English and he agreed. Then he got a funny look in his eyes, grabbed some paper, and started drawing. In about ten minutes he had this picture of a bunch of Rockwell kids (you know, long necks, freckles, ears sticking out, unlaced tennis shoes) standing around a railway depot. Meanwhile, old Number Nine was chug-chugging in. He'd put a mouth on the train, and a pair of arms coming around the side, and it was stuffing itself with bread stuffed with, like, tuna salad or something. He called it, "Munching Our Sandwiches, the Train Came Into the Station."

I laughed fit to bust, and so did the others when they saw it. After that, we started doing that kind of thing off and on. That is, David and whoever was in would sit around and swap stories and jokes and David would do cartoons.

A bit later, Karen started bringing her guitar, and she'd do a song or two every once in a while. And some time around then, so as not to be left out, I'd tell a half-remembered, half-made-up Hungarian fairy tale.

We've kept that kind of thing up, though we don't do it as much as we used to. But the funny thing is, when I'd tell one of the fairy tales, usually stretching it out over the course of a week or two, the tale would tend to creep into whatever painting I was working on. Strange isn't it?

2. *The Transfiguration*

Drawing is at the heart of everything. Drawing is so pure. You can put as much or as little into it as you want, be as real or as abstract as you want, as detailed or as spare as you want. This is true of everything, I guess, but when you're sitting there with illustration board and a pen or a pencil or a conti crayon it hits you. Then you get to make all the decisions, and all the decisions are shape.

Perspective? What's perspective except choosing which of an object's shapes you want to look at? Well, all right, it's a little more than that. But not much.

It was with my sketchbook that I discovered for the first time how beautiful a form could be, devoid of color, background, or really, any content. Pure form. The shape of a tree. A woman. Or, hell, a cloud or a car.

It was with my sketchbook that I discovered that trying to capture form revealed content, in one way or another. It was with my sketchbook that I began to understand mass. It was with my sketchbook that I began to understand that I could explore my own feelings merely by asserting the lines that nature had supplied for me.

When I work from an empty canvas and *go,* I do my sketching in oil with a brush, but for all that, it's still sketching.

3. *The Tribute Money*

I was in the studio the next day at the crack of noon. Dan was up on the balcony staring at a canvas and probably scowling, and Karen was staring at the acrylic on masonite in front of her and probably puckering her lips. When we were first setting up the studio, Karen managed to acquire a restaurant corner booth, and she sets her paintings up on the table along with her implements and some astrology tables that I don't think she takes as seriously as she pretends to.

She broke off and turned around when I came up behind her. Her long, dimpled face with basset-hound eyes was framed, first by her dark, dark hair, then by the grayish background against which she was painting a red snake, coiling. I looked more closely at the masonite and saw light sketch marks, outlining a bird fascinated by the snake. An interesting subject, and I got the impression that she was going to do some fun things with the background, but eventually she's going to have to do people.

Or maybe not. Who am I to judge?

She said, "Howdy, Greg. The Monster, I see."

I nodded, resisting the temptation to look around at what I'd done the night before. I suddenly wondered whether the whole studio had spent the last year debating when and if I was going to haul the thing out. Was there an office pool? Who'd won?

Karen said, "You're just tearing into it, then?" and I had a momentary flash of irrational annoyance.

I said, "For now. I might change my mind."

She said, "Want a reading?"

"On what?"

"On how the painting will turn out."

I laughed. "Sure, if you use the Morgan deck."

To my surprise she said, "All right," and fiddled around for a bit inside her purse and came up with it. She moved the canvas to the side, swept off an area with her hand, and unwrapped the deck. If you aren't familiar with the Morgan deck, I'll just say that it's to tarot what Andy Warhol's work is to art.

I won't bore you with the details, but the reading was fun. The overall atmosphere was "tomato, potato, eggplant," the mood passing away was, "this is central headquarters," and the outcome was, "This may not be a perfect circle, but it's a perfect whatever it is." That last was especially appropriate, I thought, except that it was an appropriate outcome for all my paintings.

I thanked her for the reading and she got back to work. I climbed the stairs to Dan's area, which is always more of a mess than mine but no one bugs him about it. I stepped over empty Orange Soda cans and looked at his current project. Six different sketches in six different sizes were taped up on a couple of extra easels on each side of the canvas, and they all looked good. The canvas itself was spectacular, even in this incomplete state. He called it, "Lost," and I decided that was a good name for it. It was a street scene, based on downtown, and if you looked at it casually the name didn't make any sense, because the movement was so strong that you were certain the two guys knew where they were going, but if you looked at them carefully, and studied their eyes, it chilled you. He was done with the figures (he'd finished with the models a week before) and was working on the background now, and if I knew Dan he would leave it vague and nebulous, making it sort of an Everycity. The background colors were pastels, and the colors for the figures were sharp fleshtones (I know that "sharp fleshtones" sounds funny, but that's what they were; Dan actually told me how he did that) with black and white for their clothes. If I'd tried that the figures would have stuck out like they didn't belong there, but Dan has a way with wet-on-wet of blending in things that ought not to blend, and I could already see that they fit right in.

As I watched, he gave the little settling of his shoulders that meant he was going to rest for a moment. He brought his chin down to his chest, then leaned his head back, and shook it. Sympathetic tension in my own neck eased as he did this.

He turned around to watch me studying his painting. His eyes are brown and have the gleam you get from doing too many drugs, although he's never done much of anything as far as I know, and certainly doesn't now. There were traces of perspiration above the bump of his nose, and his almost invisible eyebrows were damp beneath the hints of creases you can see even when his forehead isn't wrinkled. His hair is short and thin and the color of plywood.

I said, "It's looking good," meaning the painting, not the hair.

"Thanks."

"Bobby and I are hitting The Revue tonight. Wanna come along?"

"I'll pass," he said, as he always did.

I shook my head. "How can you paint if you don't dance? It isn't natural."

"It's a gift," he said.

I called down to Karen. "How about you? The Revue?"

"'Betcha," she said.

I said, "Good," and meant it. She dances better than she paints.

Then she called up, "Oh, yeah, did Robert talk to you about the rent?"

"I've got my share," I said, wishing the subject hadn't come up. If Debbie would bitch about it I'd probably feel better.

Dan leaned on the railing so he could talk to both of us. Karen came closer and stared up. Dan said, "David and I were talking yesterday."

I said, "Yeah?"

Dan said, "What do you people think about trying a show."

I said, "My uncle has a barn."

He said, "I'm serious."

I was about to ask what had changed since last year, when Karen said, "We thought about that last year. We need to know someone will at least look at the stuff or there isn't any point."

So I said to her, "They can't notice us if we aren't doing anything."

Karen gave me a funny look, but I was rewarded by Dan saying, "That's what I was thinking. We're doing some interesting stuff here. If we can just get noticed, we might be able to sell something."

"Where are we supposed to find the money?" asked Karen.

Dan chewed on his lip. "I was thinking about going back to temp work."

"No!" The outburst was mine, and it startled me. After a moment I said, "I don't think it's worth it, you know?"

Dan said, "Let's find out what Robert and David say

about the show first. Then we'll see."

Karen got back to work and I stepped over and studied one of Robert's throwaways, this one of the back of his left hand, one of his favorite subjects. At first glance, it was just resting on the paper, flat, but if you looked again, there was a certain tension in the fingers and on the back of the hand, as if he were clawing at something, or desperate.

I said, "You know, Dan, sometimes I think Rob does his best work when he just dashes something off. Have you seen this?"

"I noticed it earlier. Yeah, it's nice."

He wouldn't commit to anything else. He turned back to his work. I had no choice but to turn to mine.

4. *The Battle of San Romano*

I took my first look at the Monster since I'd left it the night before. The weird green in the upper middle brightened to a more forceful tint to the right and a straight mix to the left, to a darker and more suggestive tone. I had, indeed, had to set the canvas on the floor to work on the top, but I eventually had the whole background color. Then I'd attacked the left side with a rag with turpentine on it and wiped out sections, pretty much at random, then left before looking at it.

I studied the results from a distance.

Well, there was nothing especially pretty about it, but it *was* sort of interesting. If I were of the school that awards fifty brownie points for interesting, I could crop it, call it done, and put it in a show. The wiped-out sections had some definite forms beginning to appear. I avoided looking at them and thought about the way the colors merged and shifted, and decided I liked it. I was certainly going to have to do something more vibrant, but it was all right so far.

I moved a little closer, and a skull jumped out at me, in masses formed partly by the wiped out areas and partly by an excessively heavy application of the dark green.

A skull? Well, I wasn't real interested in doing William Blake, but it's always possible to start with a skull and put a face around it. I moved a little closer and decided that there were mountains in the background, and probably three figures all together. The skull was close to the middle. The figure that would have to be built around it would be big enough that balance shouldn't be a problem. I wondered what sort of face it would end up with. With all of the elements that were popping into my head, I was going to have to be careful to avoid cluttering the thing, even on a canvas this size. The central figure would have to dominate the other two.

But that was for later. I studied the skull and wondered about the figure I'd build around it. The discussion with Robert came back, and it occurred to me that I was looking at Uranus. Well, maybe. Who were the other figures, and what were they doing? There had to be movement, and, in fact, as I looked at the wash of colors I'd put down, I could already sense movement in it.

I came closer and found that I was next to the table and palette. I picked up the latter and started dabbing on paints, hardly glancing down as I did. Palette and brushes ready, I found the spot to work on. I wasn't yet ready for a model of Uranus, or to even decide who the others were. I had something here and I needed to find out what it was.

I built up a bright blue, lightened it with some white, and other than that left it alone. I selected an eight-inch brush and began work on the area to the right of the skull, looking for a hint of the mass that would balance the figure that had to be there.

After a while I realized I'd stopped, so I took a look at it, saw where I wanted to go, and put a few folds into what was going to become a robe. Another figure would have to go there, and it was facing Uranus. I stepped back and decided it was too small, which meant I was going to have to make it bigger or add another mass to the right of it.

The notion hit me of having a darker green emerge from the very light green, and blend with it. Some time before Dan had been discussing large canvases in general, and had made a remark to the effect that you could have strong lines and delicate shadings in the same piece if you were careful. So I'd be careful, and shade from green to green.

Green? Nature. Forests. Pheasant hunting with my Uncle Mike. Hunter. Greek. Artemis. Bingo!

I mixed viridian with white and black and ochre and got a slightly darker version of the color I'd started with and began the process of bringing out what was implied.

A long time later I stopped. Form had suggested content and I was done messing around. It was time to decide on the ultimate direction, and moreover, time to look for models.

5. *The Garden of Delights*

The next day there came a man who wore a gown of blue. He stopped at the thicket and said, "Is one of you Csucskári the Gypsy?"

Well, Csucskári stood up and bowed in the manner of Gypsies, with his back leg bent and his hands curled to his sides, and he said, "I am Csucskári the Gypsy."

"Well," says the counselor, "my three hundred and sixty-five companions and I told the king what you said, and he seemed pleased enough, but we have thought and thought and we don't know how to find the tallest tree in the world, or a rope long enough to go around the world."

"Well," said Csucskári, "if three hundred and sixty-six of you couldn't find these things, I daresay I'd be at a loss to better your work."

The counselor's face fell at these words, and he seemed so unhappy that Csucskári said, "Come now, there is certainly something we can do. If we cannot find the tallest tree in the world, we will use Mount Szaniszlo, for surely its branches are in the sky and its roots deep in the ground. And as for the rope, well, if the River Tündér doesn't go all around the world, at least it must come close, for I've never met anyone who has seen the end of it. So you take us to the king and we'll sign a contract with him, and then we'll be off to set the sun, the moon, and the stars up in the heavens where they belong."

That was enough for the counselor, so he led the Gypsies back down the road and over seven seas and six mountains and five rivers and four deserts and through three valleys and two villages until they came to the kingdom, where they were led into a palace that was so big a barn would have been lost in it.

The counselor led them through seven halls and up six stairs and through five libraries and four kitchens and three pantries and two dining rooms until they were before the king.

"Good day, Sire Your Majesty My Liege Lord, I am Csucskári the Gypsy, and these are my brothers Holló and Bagoly, and we are here to place the sun, the moon, and the stars in heaven."

"That's good," said the king. And he called for pen and paper. But before they came, Csucskári held his little finger up in the air, and with it he wrote out a contract in glowing gold letters, so the contract burned where the king and his three hundred and sixty-six counselors could see it. The contract said that if Csucskári and his brothers should succeed in putting the moon and the sun and the stars in the heavens, they would have half the kingdom to share and Csucskári would marry the king's daughter, and Csucskári signed it before their eyes.

When the pen and paper arrived, the letters burned themselves into the paper where they appeared as gold ink, and the king signed it with pen, below where Csucskári had signed it.

Then Csucskári borrowed seven swords from seven of the king's hussars, and on the seven hilts of the seven swords made his brothers swear to follow him without question in everything that came after. This done, they took their leave of the king and set out on their mission.

6. *Christ Walking on the Waters*

The first thing I notice is form. I don't think it's just me, either. I mean, I'm not the only one who ever looks at clouds, am I? A lot of people do that, even if there isn't any rain threatening. When you look up at the sky, are you thinking about water vapors and air masses? If you are, maybe I *am* weird.

But I look at the shape, just to see if it's especially interesting or pretty. Most of the time there's nothing worth seeing, but I look anyway. I don't think that makes me strange.

We all notice shapes. You recognize a friend by the shape of his face. You know your car by its shape and color. The hard part is to get past those shapes. It's fine for me to enjoy looking at clouds, but if I were a meteorologist I'd have to know what they meant. If I were a shrink I'd have to get inside the guy's head. If I were a mechanic, just seeing the shape of the car wouldn't be enough.

With painting, appearance is all you have to work with; but if you stop there, well, I don't think you're doing as much as you could. I know the Impressionists did some great work that way, but that's only what they said they were doing; and if you've ever listened to Robert talking about his pen and ink work, you'd know enough to ignore most of what an artist says about what he's doing. I suppose that includes me, too, but let's not get into that.

No, the real questions are: What do those forms mean? And, aside from that, what do they say?

So I let the forms emerge as they will, but I'm thinking about what they mean and how they go about their business. I can't *force* a meaning on them, like Hunt or Rossetti did, but I can work for an effect in tone and color and know that I'm putting myself into the painting. I once asked Dan why he'd never done a self-portrait, and he said everything he did was a self-portrait, and I think I know what he means.

Sometimes I'm afraid I can only paint myself ugly.

Bones?

CHAPTER
·THREE·

1. THE DEATH OF PROCRIS

THE SALE I MENTIONED earlier came from the first and (so far) only time I deliberately set out to do an erotic painting. I'm still rather proud of that one. In fact, I have a print of it up in our apartment—the only work of mine I've done that with. Of course, it helps that I used Debbie as one of the models.

It was an outdoor scene, with rolling hills in the background. (I drove out of town and set up near Three Oaks Hill to get it.) It was basically two figures, seen in profile, facing each other on a blanket. The effect I was going for, has to do with the hill in the background. I gave it a strong line, and the angle of the hill, and *only* the angle of the hill, suggested that her head was placed just right to go for his crotch. I mean, I'd done nudes before, and even pretty nudes outdoors, but I was trying to be as suggestive, and still as subtle, as I possibly could.

When I saw the movie, "This is Spinal Tap" I had a great temptation to title the thing "Lick My Love Pump," but I resisted and called it "Nudes at Three Oaks Hill." A couple of friends of mine really flipped out for it, and I set a price of two hundred dollars on it, and a friend of a friend of a friend (or something like that) bought it so fast I'm sure I could have gotten more. But I don't mind. For me it was a very ambitious bit of work, and it succeeded, and looking at the print consoles me when I'm depressed, which is most of the rest of the time when I'm trying ambitious things.

2. *St. Jerome in his Study*

Let me put it this way; if I were a comedian I'd want to do more than just make people laugh. A lot of the cheapest slapstick can make you laugh if your sense of humor works that way, and race jokes and that kind of thing have been making people laugh for years, but there are comedians who seem to do more than that.

They say, "You know, life really *is* pretty funny, if you stop and look at it. Here, let me help you look at it so you can see how funny it is." Then they show you something you're familiar with already, but skewed just enough so you can really see it, and you go, yeah, he's right, that *is* pretty funny when you stop and think about it. I mean, those guys are out there, you know? Cosby, George Carlin, hell, Mark Twain did that when he was being funny, didn't he? On the other hand, you can be as insightful as you want, but if you don't make people laugh you're wasting your time and theirs.

Can you see it coming? I feel the same way about art. I want to do more than just paint a pretty picture; I want there to be some substance to it, something about life, about nature, about people. I want someone to be able to look at one of my paintings more than once; more than twice even, and continue to find things in it. I want people to say, "Yeah, I've seen that, but I didn't really notice it was like that before."

But you can't just impose "meaning" and "significance" onto a painting, like adding vodka to a punch. It's either in you or it isn't. The joke is, though, that you can't know if it is or it isn't unless you work at it. You work at it by trying, as hard as you can, to *feel* something for your subject, to put yourself into it, and remember, all the time, that if you can't paint a picture that people want to look at you're just wasting your time, no matter how loudly you insist that you just aren't *understood.*

Even if the critics agree with you.

Or else you don't bother, and admit to yourself that you're always going to be second rate.

3. Bacchus and Ariadne

I trained Sunday morning in the weird class (special, all styles welcomed) which was fun. I did some slow sparring with a tae kwon do red belt (I don't know what the equivalent of a red belt would be in our style) and did all right, and did some of what passes for sparring among tai chi types and that was very strange, involving just sort of pushing each other's hands around to try to throw the other guy off balance. I also got to see Jamie do some serious sparring with someone I didn't know from a competing Shotokan school, and that was a lot of fun.

Jamie is one of those guys I could watch for hours.

His technique is not only quick, but when he scores it's like there's this instant freeze-frame, where everything seems to stop and there's an instant of timelessness, where the beauty and power takes your breath away. I'd love to paint that. I'm going to, someday.

When I came back I was ready to work. Everyone was there, which is a little unusual for a Sunday, but nobody was actually working, which evened things out.

"Hi, Greg. Your ears stopped ringing yet?" This from David.

I said, "What?" He laughed. I said, "Your feet stopped twitching?"

"Never." David's area was always spotless, which may be why, back when we were setting up the place, he ended up nearest the door. David himself is pretty big, and over the course of a year he fluctuates between being beautifully built and being slightly flabby, depending on whether he's doing his body building. Right now he's in between. At its worst, the fat never goes to his face, which is kind of an olive color with hollow cheeks and high brows, and surrounded by honest-to-god black shoulder-length ringlets that he parts in the middle. What Karen would call a hunk, and, in fact, she'd said so to me once when we were discussing the physical attributes of the studio members. Present company excepted. David was wearing jeans and a faded blue tee-shirt that had had its arms amputated and had once said, "Cornell." When he's in shape it is a very impressive shirt.

I stared over David's shoulder at a half-finished pen and ink that he'd abandoned a week ago. He said, "What d'you think?"

"I like it. Who is it?"

"My mother."

"Really? Gee. Gonna call it 'Harmony in—' "

"No."

"Just as well. Are you going to do more with her

hair?"

"Should I?"

"Well, it looks kind of dead."

"Ummmm. Yeah, I suppose so. Any ideas?"

"Well, she's your mother, but . . ." I found a pencil on the table and sketched in some hints of escaping strands to the side and put in some suggestions of puffing up in front.

"I see what you mean," he said. "Thanks."

It's always more fun to mess with someone else's work than your own.

David said, "What do you think about this show idea?"

"It sounds good if we can do it."

Robert came over as we talked. "You mean," he put in, "if we suddenly get rich."

I shook my head. "It never stops bothering me to realize how many of my problems could be solved by having large amounts of cash. For a retired hippy, it has to be the ultimate tragedy."

"Dig it," said Robert, a trace of irony in his voice.

"When did you retire?" asked David.

I suggested that he could shut up any time now.

He said, "I've got about six or seven pieces I'd be willing to put up."

"You including that still-life with the funny shadows?" I asked.

"I was thinking about it."

"Good. I really like that."

"Thanks."

"I've got a couple I could put in," said Robert.

I dropped my voice. "What do we do about Karen?"

David shrugged. Robert said, "The thing with the horses isn't too bad."

I said, "It isn't too good."

"Look—"

"I know. All right. And everything Dan's done for the last two years could go in."

"Yeah," said Robert. "Both of them."

"He's not that bad."

"I suppose. I like where you're going with the Monster, by the way."

"I haven't looked at it today. I guess it's all right so far, but I'm getting to the crunch now."

"You going to work off photos?"

"No. I've got Cindy coming in to pose."

"When?"

I looked at my watch. "Any minute."

"Too bad. I was hoping you could do more of the story."

I didn't say anything, although I was pretty pleased.

David started working on the pen and ink of his mother, which fact counted as my good deed more than the help I'd given him on it. Robert and I wandered away toward Karen's area, where she was carrying on an animated conversation with Dan. She was wearing jeans and a black pullover sweater. When she turned around, I saw that it did nice things for her hair and complexion. I will say she knows how to dress, although I hadn't realized it at first. She broke off and said, "Howdy, gentlemen. Recovered?"

"Mostly," said Robert.

"You need more exercise," I told him. "For instance, you could join—"

"Give it up, Greg."

"*Any*way," said Dan, and Karen turned back to him.

"Oh, right. What I mean is that Da Vinci was only the best known. Masaccio, Brunelleschi, there were a lot of painters who were also, like, engineers, poets, tacticians, whatever. Good ones, too."

Dan said, "What's your point?"

"Have you read any Joyce?"

"I tried to read *Ulysses* once."

"I know I'm not going to catch you on music, but what do you know about architecture?"

"I've read Tom Wolfe's thing."

"That's something, anyway."

"I still don't see what you're driving at."

"I do," put in Robert. "It's only in this century that you have so many artists—I should say painters—who don't really know anything about any art but their own. It used to be that if you were into the arts, then you were into all the arts. But now everyone has tunnel vision."

"Right," said Karen. "Tunnel vision. That's what it is."

Dan said, "I'd like to know your source for that."

I said, "If I start getting involved in this, I don't think I'll stop. Excuse me, folks."

Karen said, "Actually, Greg, wait a minute. Since so many of us are here."

Robert said, "Yeah?"

"About this show idea."

I said, "Yeah?"

"You really think we ought to do it?"

I said, "If we can. Why're you down on the idea?"

She was quiet for a moment, then she said in a low voice, "I don't really think I have anything good enough to go in."

I tried not to stare. Son of a bitch! After a bit I said, "What about the one with the horses?" and I could feel Robert looking at me.

Karen said, "Yeah, I suppose."

I felt the draft from the opening door and saw Cindy walk in. She was all smiles, and wore a light green jumpsuit. I thought it was rather amusing that she chose to wear green; I hadn't told her what the painting was going to be. Cindy had hair as dark as Karen's, but with a bit more of a curl. Her complexion was dark and she was small and, say, trim, with a really fine figure all the way around, and a wonderfully expressive face. I'd met her at the "U" where she was a theater major (she was now, naturally, a typist) and she'd modeled for me quite a bit, and for Dan a couple of times. If you want a good-looking woman who will challenge your ability to do facial expressions, get Cindy.

I received a hug&kiss when she came up. She wasn't wearing anything at all under the jumpsuit. Hot damn. ("What?" You cry. "You're about to sit her down, naked, and stare at her for several hours, and yet you're excited because she isn't wearing any underclothes?" It doesn't make sense to me either. But since when are hormones supposed to make sense?)

She exchanged a few words with Karen, and Dan came up and I left them while I set up my screens, which I should have done while I was waiting for her. She came over as I finished. I handed her the robe and left her there. I got a diet Coke and a real one from the machine and poured the diet into a plastic cup.

Robert came up to me beside the machine and said in a low voice, "Why did you bullshit Karen?"

"What do you mean?"

"Why didn't you tell her what you really thought instead of giving her that crap about the horse picture?"

"Why didn't you?"

"You're the one who's down on everything she does. If you feel that way—"

"If I feel that way what? I'm supposed to go up to her and say, 'Hi, Karen, I just thought I'd let you know that your work stinks.' "

"Well, it's better than lying to her."

"Who lied?"

"Don't split hairs."

"Look, Robert, it isn't going to do anyone any good if I just go putting down everything in sight. She—"

"You think she doesn't pick up on how you feel?"

I felt a dropping sensation in my stomach. "Do you think she does?"

"Probably."

"Oh, shit."

Cindy was calling from behind the screen. I walked over to it.

"What?"

"I said I'm ready."

"Okay."

Robert went back upstairs. I handed Cindy the cup.

"How's Debbie?" she asked.

"Huh? Oh. All right. She's still checking baggage for Fly-By-Night Airlines."

"I guess it's a living. Where do you want me?"

I indicated the grey cushions, and started assembling my implements of creation. I said, "I'm still feeling guilty about her."

"Guilty? Why?"

"She says she wants to keep photography as just a hobby, but it doesn't seem fair for her to support me so I can do art, and she has to fight rush hour twice a day and she hardly gets to work on what she wants to. I don't think she's been in the darkroom for a month."

"It's her choice," said Cindy, and she took off the robe and sat down on the cushions.

4. *A Knight's Dream*

I looked at the Monster and started trying to get a feel for how to pose Cindy. I stepped back a bit, then up again, scowled, grimaced, and said, "Look to your right and put your left leg out. Okay, now look more forward, and put out your right arm."

"Who am I?"

"Artemis, the Huntress. You know, the Greek version

of Diana."

"Oh, wow. Really? I like that. What am I doing?"

"Ummmm . . . I'm not sure."

"Great. I'll just make it up then."

One quick glance from the painting to Cindy and I knew she was going to be the center of interest, whatever I did with the other two figures. She was so striking, sitting with her head thrown back, that she almost jumped right on to the canvas. I said, "Don't move."

She didn't answer, a skill that comes from experience. I started mixing paints. I *had* to get this down. She was so vibrant, giving off so much energy. How can people work from photos? I know some painters do, and I've even done it myself, but when you can get a model like Cindy, how can you be happy with a flattened out image on a page?

I started painting, and, within half an hour, I remembered the answer. She was in front of me, and I held the brush, and it would go just where I told it, but I couldn't make it right. The line of her left arm and shoulder, with her hand resting on the cushions, was a living allegory of grace, and it wouldn't go down. I painted over it three times, and still wasn't happy.

And there's a limit to how often you can cover over an oil before the sheer amount of paint will change the effect beyond recognition.

I could have sketched it in first, but I'd thought I could get away with starting in with the oils and it was too late now. I studied Cindy for signs of fatigue, but she seemed to be doing fine. I'd have pinned a medal on her but it would have drawn blood. I knew she couldn't last forever, and once she moved I might not be able to get that pose back. Damn damn damn.

Okay. I took a deep breath and stepped back to study her and think about it before trying again.

5. *The Creation of Adam*

Csucskári and his brothers left the palace and started walking. They came to a high cliff, and Csucskári led them along a path to the bottom. After a while Holló said, "Well, Csucskári, where are you taking us?"

"I don't know," said Csucskári.

"What?" said Bagoly. "You don't know where you are taking us?"

"That is true, my dear brothers," says Csucskári, "I don't know where I am taking you. That is why you must trust me."

They came to a river and Csucskári led them over it on the rocks so they wouldn't fall in."

"But," says Holló, "are you looking for something?"

Csucskári says, "Yes, I am looking for something."

"Well then," says Bagoly, "what is it you're looking for?"

"I don't know," says Csucskári. "That is why you must trust me."

They came to a pasture, and Csucskári led them around the herd so the bull wouldn't see them.

"But, when you find it, will you do something?" asks Holló.

"Yes, then I'll do something," says Csucskári.

"But what will you do?" asks Bagoly.

"I don't know," was the answer. "That is why you must trust me."

Then Holló said, "How can we trust you when you don't know where you're taking us, or what you are looking for, or what you will do when you find it?"

"You can trust me because I have led you down a cliff, and over a river, and past a bull, and you have come to no harm. I suppose that is worth something."

Well, his brothers saw the wisdom of this and agreed readily enough, and soon they came to the edge of a big, black, wild forest.

Then Holló said, "Do we enter this forest, brother, or must we go around?"

Csucskári considered this, and said, "I must look around carefully, to see where we should go." And he looked around, and soon he saw the glint of gold high up in an oak. (You must not ask me how there could be a glint with no sun or moon or stars to make it. I don't know, but I know there was the glint because I saw it.)

Well, quick as thought, Csucskári was up the tree. Sure enough, one of the leaves was made of gold, and there was writing on it in red ink. Csucskári came back down the tree and showed the leaf to his brothers.

"Well, Csucskári, what does it say?" asked Holló.

"It says, 'If you wish to place the sun, the moon, and stars in the sky, you should first beware of the great boar who is coming to rip you to pieces.' "

"What?" cried Bagoly. "A great boar is coming to rip us to pieces? We are lost!"

"Well," says Csucskári, "I guess it is time to decide what to do."

6. *Sacra Conversazione*

Starting a painting is slow going, and nerve wracking, but it's also fun. Getting through the bulk of it means dealing with problems that can be more or less difficult, but don't really stop the work, and finishing the painting may be hard, but I'm so fired up by then it doesn't usually feel like work.

But there is a point where I'm always stuck. The thing that stops me is different every time, but it always comes at the same point in the project; somewhere after the beginning but before I'm a quarter of the way through it. It's so consistent that I've wondered about it a great deal, but I haven't come up with any good answers.

My best guess is that at the beginning I'm painting from excitement for the new project, so I don't think about it, and, after the crises, the hard decisions are made. But somewhere in there I have to decide what I'm doing.

My brain, I guess, isn't the most artistic part of me. Whenever it goes into action I slow down. I wish I could paint a picture from feel, all the way from beginning to end, but I guess it will just never be. At some point I have to make the decision of where I'm going and what I'm doing. The only thing worse is when I stop and ask myself, why *this* subject, why *this* approach instead of some other?

I've never come up with a good answer for that one.

Bones?

CHAPTER
• FOUR •

1. *THE BURIAL OF COUNT ORGAZ*

ONE CHRISTMAS, when I was about six or seven, I got a book called *Washington's America*, which was mostly about the Revolutionary War. I don't know who wrote it, and I remember little about the writing other than the accounts of a few battles, which I liked. Mostly I remember the pictures.

I would recognize any of them, and I've never run across them again, so I guess they weren't considered great works of art even for their day; but I loved them. The inside of the front cover had this incredible scene with massed British troops using bayonets on Colonials, and I can still remember one American in a white blouse, looking up at a soldier whose bayonet had pierced his hand as well as the arm of someone prostrate below him. The pleading expression on his face as he stared up at the soldier still haunts me. The painting still haunts me. I could *feel* the tension; I could almost smell the black powder, and hear the pandemonium of battle. I was six or seven years old, and now I'm pushing thirty, and I can still remember that picture, and a few others.

The revelation came about fifteen years ago. I don't know what brought that book to mind, but I was thinking about it, and it suddenly hit me that someone had painted that picture. A guy just like me had sat down and just painted it.

I was at school at the time, in the cafeteria eating something called mashed potatoes and gravy. I got up and made a dash for my locker, got some paper, slipped into an empty room, and started trying to reconstruct that painting.

I couldn't really come close, but I did get a battle scene and I kind of liked the way the smoke came up off someone's rifle, and the angle of someone else who was knocked backward when a shot hit him. I've since been told that when you're hit with a lead ball from a flintlock rifle you collapse from shock more than fall backward, but so what?

Up until then, I'd just sat through the art classes, and I'd never been especially noticed. After that I started really trying.

I still didn't get especially noticed, but by then we were doing things like pottery, which didn't interest me. Years later I saw a white Japanese vase without a trace of decoration that brought tears to my eyes, but never mind. I spent a lot of time drawing on my own, which I hadn't done since grade school. I mostly did battles, and I didn't show them to anyone.

But the face of that colonial haunted me. I wanted to capture something like that. I didn't understand why, and maybe I still don't, but I spent more and more time working on faces. Faces are what I'm most interested in, especially faces of people in the middle of doing something.

I wish I could find that stupid book again.

2. *A Young Man Leaning Against a Tree Among Roses*

Things haven't been easy on Debbie. She claims that she doesn't mind not doing much art, but I don't believe her. That I don't believe her probably makes things worse. I suspect she convinced herself that she could be satisfied by the romance of supporting an artist—of creating through me. It makes me kind of uncomfortable now, though it was flattering two years ago. She's finding out that it doesn't work that way, and trying like hell to deny it, so we're probably in for rough times.

But we have the darkroom, so when she's ready, I suppose I could get a day-job to support her. Or maybe I couldn't. I guess we'll see.

Over the last two or three years I've done a complete flip-flop in my attitude toward photography. I used to think, and say loudly and often, that it wasn't real art, because, despite a few mostly mechanical things in the darkroom, all you needed was a good eye and minimal technique. I'd seen some absolutely gorgeous work, but that didn't change my opinion. I'd been told that the darkroom work is more than minimal, but that didn't change my opinion. I'd been told that, with 35mm film, the selection process is the art, but that didn't change my opinion. I'd been told that timing and lens and film selection are no easy tasks, but that didn't change my opinion either.

I don't know exactly what made me reconsider; maybe a combination of all of the above and knowing Debbie, who is a very good photographer. In any case, now I wonder if it isn't one of the most pure arts. If you stay away from tricks (Debbie does some developing and double-exposure tricks that I don't like, but never mind), all you have to work with is nature, which means you have to find beauty and meaning in nature itself; you can't impose it from the outside.

There's a photographer friend of Debbie's named Fred who always says, "The lens points both ways," and I guess that's what I didn't realize at first. I should have, because any fool can see what a paint brush or pen does. I'm not about to pick up a camera myself, if it isn't my medium; but what is so fascinating about art is when you have to look outside yourself to find what is inside, and with a camera, the *only* way to show what's inside is to point to something outside—you can't fool yourself into thinking you're making it all up. You find something in nature that expresses something about you; you find something inside of yourself that expresses something about nature.

And that's what we're all about, isn't it?

3. *Venus, Cupid, Folly and Time*

I was alone in the studio early Monday afternoon.

I walked around the place, just pacing and staring at everyone's work, and I decided I felt good. I love being the only one in the studio, either working or not. For one thing, that way I can indulge in my private vice of Led Zeppelin. Don't tell anyone, all right?

The problem with my Artemis had solved itself at the cost of only a few pints of blood (metaphorically speaking) and sweat (almost literally). It was obvious in retrospect. I had gone back to the face and captured her expression (and gotten it *right*, I was sure of that), then the torso, and the shoulder and arm had just followed as they had to. The hands weren't even difficult. Now, less than twenty-four hours later, it was hard to remember why it seemed impossible at the time. I keep rediscovering things I learned years ago.

I decided I'd have to be careful how I dressed the figure; I remember a painting at the art institute by one of those dead French guys that had Diana in a gown that wouldn't have lasted ten seconds in the woods, and that sort of thing has always bothered me.

I put a tape of Led Zeppelin's on, then went upstairs and stared at Dan's street scene and felt both humble and excited. God, he's good. I'd like to be able to do that. I wondered if it would be frustrating to be that good and have no one realize it. But then, Dan doesn't seem to think he's that good either. He talks of how he just splashes on the paint, and about how Whistler would spend weeks and months and even years on a simple portrait. So what? You spend as long as you need to on any piece, and that's that. Sheesh.

That's what I'd tell the art critic from *Art in America* who would fly down to interview me. "Mister Kovaks," he would say, and I'd stop him to correct his pronunciation. He'd blush. "Sorry, Mister . . . Kovawch?"

"Something like that. It's all right." Magnanimous. "Call me Greg."

"All right—then." He wouldn't be able to bring himself to use my first name. He'd be too much in awe of me. "Were you aware that you were starting a new school of art?"

I'd make kind of an embarrassed smile. "Well, I guess I'd have to say no. I mean, I'm still not aware of it. I'm just painting what I see. If you want genius, look at these." And I'd show him some of Dan's works. He'd stare at them for a long time, from different distances and angles, and nod slowly.

"I see what you mean," he'd say. "These are unquestionably great works, and I can see where he's influenced you. But there's something indefinable missing in these that you have. Your paintings exist on so many levels."

"I'm glad," I'd say. Straightforward. "I wasn't really trying to say anything deep, but at the same time I think it's important that you do something more than just paint a decoration."

"But in a sense, your works *are* decorative, too. I mean, the sheer *beauty* of, for instance, your 'West Side Twilight' is astounding."

"Well, thanks. I have to say that one came out pretty much the way I wanted it to. I'm still not quite satisfied with the movement of some of the cars, but—"

"Not satisfied!" he'd cry, "But—"

The door opened and I was pulled rudely back to reality. That was all right; it hadn't been going that well anyway. Critics never talk about indefinable somethings; they're in the business of defining them. Robert joined me upstairs, beret and all. I said, "Hiya, Unca Bobby."

"Howdy, Greg. Slain the Monster? Or are you trying to scare it off?"

I ignored his musical judgments except to reach out and drop the volume a bit. I said, "It's actually going better than I thought it would."

"Good."

"And while we're on the subject, you've been doing some nice studies. I like them."

"You mean the hand? Be serious."

"I am. Going to start a project any time this year?"

"Yeah, I've got one coming, I think. I'm still letting

it stew."

I leaned back against the railing, looking at Dan's work. Then I stood up straight, because the railing isn't that sturdy. Robert pointed to one of the figures and said, "I have this awful urge to put a halo over his head."

For a second I was insulted on Dan's behalf, then I decided I could see what he was talking about. There *was* something almost saintly about him. Robert and I studied Dan's work together. Robert isn't in awe of Dan the way I am. I can't help feeling that this means there's something wrong with Robert, even though I know it doesn't.

It was suddenly depressing to think how out of step we were—all of us—with the art world. To think that this painting would probably never sell, and almost certainly never be appreciated, at least in our lifetimes. My sense of irony kicked in and prevented me from getting maudlin about the plight of the poor, misunderstood painter. But then, that's a cliché because sometimes there's truth in it, right?

I said, "Say, Robert?"

"Yeah?"

"Remember when we started this place?"

"No. I was on drugs at the time."

"Be serious."

"All right. What about it?"

"You and I were the ones who thought we'd never really get anywhere, remember?"

"Yeah."

I didn't say anything. Robert sat down on Dan's table, which was really an antique wooden desk that you could have set an elephant on. He said, "What is it?"

I sat down on the floor, resting my back against the railing. "I don't know. I guess, what's the point of doing all of this stuff if no one ever sees it except us and a few friends?"

"Well, yeah. That's why Dan was talking about the show."

I shook my head. "It's just that we've been doing this for, what, almost three years? You'd think *someone* would have noticed us if we were on the right track."

"Not necessarily."

"Look—"

"It isn't a matter of 'the right track.' It's *a* right track. No one ever said that the five of us are the only legit artists in the world. But," he waved his arm around the studio, "look at the pictures. Don't you think we have something?"

"Sure I do. Why doesn't anyone else?"

"Has it occurred to you that there's more involved than just producing good work? How many great musicians are there floating around who will never cut an album, just because they can't get the breaks?"

"This isn't the music business."

"No. There's at least *some* money in the music business."

"We originally said two years, and it's been almost three."

He dropped his voice. "You thinking about giving up?"

I sighed. "Thinking about it? Yeah. Want to? No. I could do things that would sell. You know, poster work, or Tim what's-his-name who wants to do a comic book with me. What I want is for someone to convince me I shouldn't."

Robert sighed. Eyes to heaven. *"Il Magnifico*, where are you when we need you?"* Eyes to Greg. "Are you ready to just throw it all out?"

"Sometimes," I told him.

He chewed on his lip. "But not until you finish your picture." He smiled. "And the story, you son-of-a-bitch."

I felt a chuckle in my throat. "Right. Not until I finish the story, at least."

4. *The Misanthrope*

The work was starting to have some substance to it. I stepped back and looked at it, trying, yet again, to get a fresh view. It was so bleeding *big*, you know? Maybe that was why I'd gone to the old, old traditions: if you're going to do something that big, you really ought to be dealing with a big subject.

No, that's silly. When Rembrandt painted the guard out on the town, it was a big subject because he made it one. Oh, well. I need to stop trying to figure myself out, and just paint.

I played with the lights a little to make sure they were hitting the whole thing evenly. I felt odd, and it took me a moment to realize that it was because I hadn't taken the screens down. I'm used to working out in the big room that's the studio; the tiny room I'd created with the screens made it seem a different place.

I left them there, though, and thought about what to tackle next. There was a whole big background that I hadn't really touched. It looked incredibly imposing. What was I going to do, anyway? It was still suggesting mountains, but what mountains? After working with Cindy I didn't want to work from photos, and I was not about to take the Monster outside—not after putting this much work in on it.

Well, I could do a Da Vinci—just make up a background out of whole cloth. That *was* a thought. Why not? I was dealing with myths, for Chrissake, why not put in a fake Olympus or something. Yeah, that could be nice, although I was going to have to be careful about not cluttering the thing, despite its size. But, sure, why not a bit of mountain back there? Snow covered, lightning crowned, but fading out in back, so it wouldn't draw attention away from my Artemis, or Uranus, or Apollo—

Apollo?

How did Apollo get in here?

I looked to Artemis's right, opposite Uranus, and I realized that, indeed, Apollo was going to have to go there.

There was a moment of indecision, between god and mountain, but I finally started building the soft grays for the background and the lightning yellow and the dirty-white of the snow. I'd have to think about Apollo. For one thing, the place he wanted to go would have the three of them on the same plane. Can you say, "boring?" I'd have to raise him up, and put him . . . how about on one knee, on a rock, holding his bow?

Sheesh! Not now, Greg.

I stared at the background, hoping for inspiration but determined to do without if I had to. Just to amuse myself and kill some time while I thought, I took a six-teenth inch brush and, in the lower right corner, painted in the little brown-eyed girl who seems to follow me from painting to painting.

Maybe she helped, I don't know. But the fire took me then, just for a little while, and I played God, raising mountains from nothing, and crowning them with snow and lightning, all in a fading away background that most viewers wouldn't even notice. I set the canvas on the floor, and brought the overcast sky to the top, then started carrying the mountain chain back to the left. I gobbed on the paint, huge thick mounds of it, just because this was oil goddamit, not acrylic, and flat is flat is flat and I didn't want flat. The hours flew by me like the eagles of Zeus.

5. *The Meat Stall*

Csucskári leapt to the tree, for a sudden fire seemed to come over him. He pulled a branch from the tree. He breathed on it and it became a spear with a glowing iron tip. Then he called, "Come on, you boar, let us play a game, one with the other, and see who is the stronger."

Well, you know how it is when a *taltos* yells, so you can bet the forest rang like the bells of Ujoltar. The old boar came up out of the forest, and it was the biggest, blackest, meanest boar Csucskári had ever seen. But it saw the spear in Csucskári's hand, and it didn't charge. It said, "So, Csucskári, you wish to place the sun, the moon, and stars up in the sky, do you? Well, I see you have a spear, and no doubt will get the better of me if we fight, so I may as well tell you what I know."

So the boar told him where to find a stream in the forest, and that if he followed the stream he would come to a cave, and inside the cave would be a sow with nine piglets. "Now Csucskári," says the boar, "you must cut open the sow, and inside her you will find a box, and inside the box are twelve wasps, which are the sun, the moon, and stars. But be a good fellow Csucskári, and when you're done, sew her belly back up, for she needs to be able to feed her nine piglets doesn't she?"

"Well," says Csucskári, "if I say I'll sew the sow, what will you tell me about dangers I'll run into on the way?" (You see, Csucskári sensed the boar wasn't telling him everything.)

"You are clever, Csucskári. Very well. You should know that there is a troll guarding the mouth to the cave, and even you, with your glowing spear, had better have a care for that troll, or he will eat you up."

Csucskári called out, "Ho! Holló and Bagoly, be sure

to wait for me here until I get back." Then he turns to the boar and says, "Since you tried to trick me, you can carry me to the cave yourself, and you'll see how I deal with the troll."

The boar wasn't too happy to hear this, but he saw that it was either that or face Csucskári's spear, so he agreed, and Csucskári mounted upon his back and the boar carried him into the forest.

6. *The Fall of the Giants*

My favorite definition of "inspiration" is: the creative unity of the conscious and the unconscious. I like that. I don't know if I understand it, but it certainly has a nice ring to it.

There are times when the picture paints itself, and I can just stand there, brush in hand, and watch it unfold. That's when painting is its most exciting, and that's what I'm going for when I do something unplanned.

You see, I admit it: I *like* my own work. I usually don't like it six months after I've finished it, but then again, a year or two after that it usually seems all right.

But you know what annoys me? It doesn't bother me when the work paints itself (or, if you like, paints me)— that's what I most love. It doesn't even bother me when I have to fight for every drop, and spend hours covering a two-inch square (like that damn shoulder) because the muse just won't visit me. No, what annoys me is that after I've finished a piece I can't tell which parts were easy and which were like pulling teeth. You'd think one or the other would be better, wouldn't you? None of my friends can tell either; I've asked them to guess and they've never even been close.

So what can you say? Maybe inspiration is overrated. Maybe hard work is overrated. Most likely I just think too much.

Bones?

CHAPTER ·FIVE·

1. *THE LUTE PLAYER*

DAVID AND DEBBIE used to go out together. They broke up before I met either of them, but they were still friends when David and I met. This was well before we set up the studio. She'd come over to David's place and take slides of his stuff for just the cost of the film and developing. Pretty soon she started doing that for me, too. She didn't say much about my paintings, but every once in a while she'd make a comment that indicated she was appreciating my work the way I most like to have it appreciated—like she was falling into the painting. She'd murmur from time to time, or point out, say, a certain use of shading and texture that would turn out to be exactly what I'd worked hardest on in that piece. You can't make an enemy out of an artist by doing that.

One day she asked me to pose. I said, "Why?"

She said, "You're good-looking, and I like the way you use your face."

I said, "Really? Wow. Sure."

It was strange being on the other side, but Debbie's good at getting models to relax—that's something I've tried to learn from her. By the time she had me nude, it didn't even seem weird. A few days later she showed me a few of the prints. I said, "Shit! I'm gorgeous."

She said, "I know."

Then I got embarrassed and she laughed and hearing her laugh I fell in love with her, though I didn't realize it then. Debbie has told me that she fell in love with me while developing the photographs. Hopeless romantics, both of us.

I asked her to pose for me, and she agreed that was fair and I tried to make her as beautiful as she'd made me, and it wasn't too hard because she was lovely from the inside out and I'd have had to work hard to hide it.

That week we saw "Days of Heaven" by Terence Malick, mostly because Debbie thinks Richard Gere is almost as sexy as Frank Langella. We went out for coffee afterwards and stayed up all night arguing about the film. Finally Debbie announced that I was absolutely hopeless, had no understanding of what film was about, was too stubborn to even try to understand the *true* potentials of the medium, and it was a complete waste of time to try to talk to me. She went on to say that she didn't understand how someone who called himself an artist could be so completely lacking in sensibilities, and asked me to at least try not to sound so sure of myself while I was spewing nonsense, because it made her feel embarrassed for me.

We moved in together a month or so later.

2. *The Artist as 'Painting'*

If I were writing a story, I'd know (I hope) how to write a clever little line to lead the reader into it. From there, maybe I'd throw in enough of the main character's history to get the reader involved, and then I could start letting the plot unfold.

Okay, that's just the same as what I do, only what I'm after is directing your eye. This is *not* one of the more difficult things about painting. I mean, I know where your eye is going to go. No? Put it this way: if I find a point on the canvas that's about four fifths of the way toward the top, and maybe two thirds of the way to the right, and I have three pairs of eyes staring at that spot, and lines from everywhere on the canvas leading into it, and then I put in a woman whose naked tits just happen to be right there, then, goddammit, I *know* where your eyes are going to be, and I don't care who you are.

Now, I'd like to think I don't have to get that, um, extreme. But the point is, I have to know where I'm leading, and I really ought to know why. That is, if I build the thing so your eye is directed to a certain spot, I have an obligation to make that spot worth looking at, as well as making the trip interesting, and building the entire canvas so it hangs together, so to speak.

3. *The Supper at Emmaus*

When I got back from training Monday evening, I brought a friend with me. Dan had put on some Mozart, turned down pretty low. But Mozart sets up a really laid-back atmosphere, and doesn't require you to listen all that hard (sorry if that's offensive; but even Dan agrees—that's why he put it on).

David looked up from the study of his mother and said, "Howdy."

I said, "David, this is Hans. Hans, David. Hans is a brown belt at the doj." I could have gone on to add that Hans is the only brown belt I know who had placed in a regional tournament. He'd come in second, and beaten a couple of shodans and nidans to do it.

Hans has the most incredible musculature I've seen outside of body-building magazines (it's worth looking at some of those, by the way). He works—I kid you not—as a bodyguard. I don't know for whom; I have the impression he does temporary assignments for whoever happens to be in town.

He's more than six feet tall, but so perfectly proportioned that he doesn't seem big. You can imagine what his chest looks like, and I think he beat those nidans mostly through intimidation. His face is, like, pure and clear and noble, and he has a short fringe of blond hair. He looks like a Greek god.

So I had no choice, know what I mean?

He looked around the studio with some interest after muttering a hello to David, who seemed a little intimidated by him, or maybe jealous. Hans was wearing a tight black tee-shirt.

I pointed out Karen, who looked at him and I knew her well enough to see the pounce instinct warming up. Dan barely glanced around and nodded. Robert wasn't especially working on anything so he came over and I introduced them.

He shook hands with Hans. "You modeling?"

"Um, I guess so," he said.

I offered Hans a Coke which he declined, but he accepted a cup of coffee (black, how can he stand it?), which proved he wasn't completely a health nut. The challenge was to keep Hans from getting embarrassed by the situation. I enlisted his help in arranging cushions for him to pose on. I tried not to look at the Monster too much, but the glimpse or two I got told me I might have something.

When the area was ready I handed Hans the bathrobe and left him behind the screen, saying I'd be back in a minute. I wandered upstairs to see what Dan was up to. He was standing a couple of steps away from his easel, studying his work. He was chewing on his lip and his face was screwed up. I said, "Problems?"

He turned to me and said, "What? Oh. Not really. I just can't figure out how strongly I want the street defined. I'll get it."

I nodded. "I'll get it" is a code-phrase, meaning, "Keep your advice to yourself," so I did.

"Yeah. There's something about working on a canvas that size. I don't know what it is—"

"It's called freedom."

I thought about that, then nodded. "I guess so. You were right. I have to keep fighting myself to keep from putting in so much little detail that the whole thing goes."

"Yeah. Do you have a subject yet?"

"Ummmm . . . yes and no. Uranus, Artemis and Apollo, but I'm not really sure where I'm going with them."

His eyes lit up, which is about the only signal that Dan gives when he really likes something. He said, "Why did you pick that?"

"I don't know. It sort of picked itself."

"What were you starting with?"

"Form and mass and color."

"You didn't have any idea?"

"Not really. Just that I wanted to work on the Monster."

"Strange."

"You should have been at The Revue last Saturday. It would have inspired you."

"Why? Were they playing Chopin?"

"They were hot."

"Oh."

"I don't understand you. You're the one who always gives me the lectures on contemporary sensibilities, and going for something that will reach people, but you only listen to music by dead guys."

"Dead guys?" It was actually David's line; whenever I talk about how Delacroix did it or something he asks why I keep bringing up dead guys. He doesn't really mean it. I think. Anyway, Dan said, "It isn't a matter of what's good, it's a matter of what I like to listen to."

"All right, and with all the contemporary painters you're always sneering at, it's just a matter of what they like to paint."

"You're the one who sneers, not me. I just don't paint the same things they do."

"Right. And you've never said or implied that anything was wrong with them." I was being ironic here, in case you didn't catch it.

Dan was starting to look irritated. He said, "That's right. I never *have* said or implied there was anything wrong with them."

"Okay, then, why don't you paint that kind of stuff yourself?"

"It isn't what I'm interested in."

"God, you're narrow."

"Why don't *you* paint that kind of stuff?"

"Because I don't think abstractionism is good art."

"God, you're narrow."

If he weren't a genius I'd kick him.

As I walked by Karen, she said, "Who's the hunk?"

"Greg. Pleased to meet you."

"You know who I'm talking about, bozo."

I said, "Karen, do you realize that if you had brought in a woman, and I said—"

"Yeah, I do," she said cheerfully. "Who is he?"

"His name is Hans. He's attached."

"Too bad. Real attached?"

"Yeah. You could go for it anyway. He might get off on the romance of dating an artist."

"Right," she said.

I said, "You'll have to move to a garret and grow a beard, though."

"Grow a beard?" said Karen. "I can't even paint a beard."

It was supposed to be funny, and I guess it was, but there was also something else there that I couldn't quite put my finger on. I wondered what had gotten into her lately. My more cynical side wondered if she'd made the mistake of looking at her own stuff. But, no, that wasn't fair or true. She isn't really bad. But I keep waiting for her to dive in over her head, take a chance, do something dangerous. And she never does.

I said, "Karen, do you have something in mind, when you start a painting? I mean, something vague and general that you're going for?"

"What do you mean?"

"I'm trying to decide if I'm the only pretentious artist in the studio. If I am, that's okay; I figure every studio needs one, but I'm curious."

She looked at me. "I still don't understand what you're asking."

I said, "Okay, when I did that West Side piece, I was thinking about how it is that where we live has an effect on our attitudes. Like, if you live in an area that's always busy, but sort of run-down, what effect does that have on you, and now that they're building it up, does that change your attitude if you live there. Do you follow me?"

"I think so."

"It isn't that I'm trying to prove something, it's more like I'm going, 'Okay, here's this interesting question, let me take a look at it.' "

Karen nodded. "I do that sometimes. With 'Two Cats,' I was trying to get at trust. But really, I'm just trying to do pictures that are worth looking at, instead of just being decorations that fit into the color scheme of a real estate office. You know, something that someone would actually want to look at for more than ten seconds."

I nodded. "That seems a worthwhile goal," I said. I wished I liked her work more. No, that's not it. I wished I *respected* her work more.

I started to ask her something else, but then I remembered that Hans was waiting for me. I went back past the screen into my area. Hans was sitting in the robe, drinking his coffee. I said, "Give me a minute, all right?"

"Sure." He seemed relieved.

I studied the canvas for a moment, first from ten feet away, then from five, then from close up. "Okay," I said. "Let's get started."

He twitched a little. I kept looking at the canvas. He made a funny kind of sigh, like he was trying to be casual, then he dropped the robe and sat down on the cushions. I glanced at him, then back at the canvas. Dealing With Uncomfortable Models Rule Thirteen: Don't stare. I gave him a couple more quick looks, like I was only trying to figure out the pose—which I was, by the way. "Okay, lean back a little. Get as comfortable as you can, because you're going to be sitting there a while."

He rearranged himself a bit. I stared at the canvas and gave him another quick glance. "Okay, stretch out your left leg. Now raise your right arm as if . . . just a minute." I found a broom and handed it to him. I knew that broom would be useful someday.

4. *Orpheus in the Underworld*

The whole thing was too dark—in color if not in mood. I built up a green with some yellow tints and used it to outline my Apollo. While it was still wet, I came at it with the most vibrant of my flesh-tones.

Artemis was the Earth (the Greeks would disagree with that, but never mind—to me, at the moment, she was the earth), so her skin tones were as real as I could make them and she gave off energy from the inside. But my Apollo would be on fire—his very skin alive and shining.

I had to rub things out with turpentine once or twice, as Apollo decided to take a higher position, and to be holding his bow at the ready, in case Uranus was still alive. I felt a brief temptation to paint in a compound bow. Behave yourself, Greg. There are times for being serious; it's okay every once in a while.

I realized that I knew the title by now, too: "The Death of Uranus." Romantics? Who they?

Anyone who knew Greek mythology would have a cow at this version of Uranus's death. I had Hans look more sharply to his right, and hold up the broom as if it were a bow, and to tighten his pectorals. I worked hard to get the musculature, but I got it, and his chin, and his brows. Yes, he was my Apollo, slaying Uranus with Artemis.

When Hans was gone I worked a little bit more on his hands, where his fingers were wrapped around the bow, and on the bow itself. Then I went over the whole figure with a gloss. I could do that three or four more times, too, and my Apollo would *shine*.

5. *Aurora*

Csucskári hung onto the boar for all he was worth,

and at last they came to a stream. The boar plunged into the stream up to his neck, but Csucskári hung on until they were on the other side. There, just as the boar had said, there was a path. They followed the path around twists and turns and over and under hills, until they were outside a cave. Here the boar stopped, and Csucskári got off its back.

"Very well, friend boar," he says. "You have brought me safely to the cave. Now you may leave if you wish, or you can stay and see how I deal with this monster."

He'd no sooner spoken than up pops an enormous troll. He was almost twice as tall as Csucskári, and had teeth the size of fingers, and his skin was hard as granite.

The troll says, "Well Csucskári, so you want to put the sun, the moon and stars up in the heavens, eh? When you were smaller than the hundredth part of a grain in your mother's womb, I knew I'd have to kill you, so you may as well put down that spear right now."

So Csucskári says, "I can see that it will be no easy matter to fight you, especially since I have with me only a spear that couldn't even pierce your skin, and since I'm tired after a long day's trials. How about if we take a rest now, so after a good sleep we can wake up refreshed and have a real test to see which one of us is the better."

The troll says, "Ho, are you trying to trick me? Well, Csucskári, it's no use, because trolls can't sleep any more than *taltos* can."

"What?" cried Csucskári. "Can't sleep? You have never slept in your life?"

"Well," says the troll, "it is true that when I was a little troll, my mother used to tell stories that would put me to sleep, but my old mother is long gone now."

"Ah," says Csucskári, "I'll tell you a story then." And, before the troll could say another word, Csucskári began telling the story of the Yak Who Visited the Monastery. Soon the troll sat down to listen. From time to time,

Csucskári would stop his tale, in the manner of the orchard-workers of the North, and he would say, "Bones?" And, time after time, the troll would answer him, saying, "Tiles," meaning he was still awake.

But at last, once when Csucskári said, "Bones?" there came no answer, and Csucskari knew that the troll had fallen asleep. Then, quick as the wind, Csucskári slipped past him and into the cave.

6. *Entering the Ark*

We see the world in light and dark much more than we think. It isn't the colors that we notice so much as it is the contrasts. All of those studies that say yellow makes you feel safe, and light blue this or that, well, I think you can put too much emphasis on them. Oh, you can play games with that sort of thing, and I've been known to do so. Use a color that makes you feel uneasy to paint a homey little scene, or a safe color to show something threatening. But you can get too much involved with tricks; you can start using them to avoid really working.

Similarly, it's easy to make a painting "striking" by using a lot of bright, garish colors. Or you can make it moody by using a lot of dark tones and playing with how the light hits the subject, like the Dutch painters did. These, too, are too easy, and miss the point (which is not to say that there is anything wrong with those Dutch guys, but this is the nineteen-eighties, and they did that already).

It's just the same as where I'm directing your eye. *Why* I want your eye to follow this or that path? *Why* do I want a dark mood, or a striking painting? Don't I need to know the reason for what I'm doing?

Some of my favorite painters (modern painters, as well as the dead guys) insist they don't think about any of this. "I'm just trying to paint a pretty picture," they cry, or the Great Cliché, "I'm just painting what I see." And some of the worst hacks in the business talk about how they want to make people feel this or that or the other.

It just doesn't make any sense. And I can't figure out why I worry about it so much, when no one else seems to. You can think about it too much, and you can think about it too little. But when you find yourself wondering if you are wondering too much, you know things have gotten completely out of hand.

Bones?

CHAPTER
· SIX ·

1. *THE GARDEN OF LOVE*

DAVID AND I HIT it off from day one. I walked into the Chapel (the big communal studio we had at the "U") one day late in spring quarter of my sophomore year, and heard Funboy Three on someone's stereo. This muscular type I didn't know, wearing black leather cap over short brown hair, looked up when I came in, sighed, and reached over to turn it down or off, but I started singing along before he could touch the switch, and that was pretty much what started us off.

I said, "Howdy. Packing up?"

He said, "Huh, what?" Then he looked around his area, and smiled. "Oh, no. I just like to keep the place clean. I can work better."

"Strange," I said, hoping he'd take it as friendly ribbing, and I guess he did.

I went over to see what he was up to. He was working with acrylics, then, and I didn't like what he was doing at all, but I resisted the urge to tell him so. It was a wash of garish colors, with no form and a lot of white paper. I figured he'd name it, "At the Bus Station," or something, and look contemptuous whenever anyone asked him why he called it that. I glanced over his shoulder once, then said, "I like your taste in music."

He said, "Huh? Oh." Then he looked embarrassed. "This isn't a real piece," he said. "I'm just playing around trying to figure out what acrylics are good for."

I said, "What do you usually do?"

"Oils or water-colors."

"Going from oils to acrylics? Isn't that backward?"

"I don't know. It's just something I've never done."

"Oh. Well, what do you think?"

"Ummm, they're pretty flat, you know? Like water-color, but you can get sharper."

I said, "Flat? I suppose, compared to oils. Acrylic is pretty much all I do."

He said. "Yeah? Got something around? I'm David Sommers, by the way." It was always, "David," too, never "Dave."

I gave him my name and led him over to my area and hauled out a painting I'd just finished, called "Sunset: Lake Coby." He said, "Holy shit. Wait a minute." He came back with an oil called "Early Morning: The Arb."

I stared at it for a minute or two, then looked at mine, and back at his. He'd been playing with the way sunlight was bouncing off the leaves, and the effects of shadow, and I had been playing with the sunlight on the waves (which is ninety percent of the reason to do a beach scene anyway). But it wasn't that—it was just such a pleasure to run into someone doing representational art when everyone around me was trying to be Jasper Johns. I said, "Brother."

He said, "Yeah."

I said, "Where did you do this?"

"There's this arboretum, about thirty miles out of town."

"I have *got* to get there."

"I'll be driving up this weekend. Wanna come along?"

"Damn straight."

"Great. I like to leave about four in the morning to catch the sunrise."

I stared at him. "Are you crazy? I couldn't get up that early if my life depended on it."

He stared back at me. "Who said anything about getting up? I just *stay* up. Hell, there's plenty to do."

I said, "Brother!"

He said, "Yeah." Then he added, "You really should use oils there, though. I mean, it isn't flat, and if you try to make it flat—"

"There've been landscapes in water color ever since—"

"That isn't the point. You'll know what I mean when you get there. There just isn't any other way to get it."

I said, "I've never worked in oils. I'm taking that class next fall."

"Well, shit, man. Time you started." He handed me a small, pre-stretched canvas, and his palette, and said, "Go for it."

I said, "Thanks. What should I do?"

He picked up the palette knife and built up a pale red. He handed me an eighth-inch brush and said, "Get it real wet." I got some viridian on it. "No," he said. "*Real* wet."

So I did, then I said, "Now what?"

"Just sketch."

"Sketch?"

"Try it."

So I did. It took me a few minutes, because the bristles were stiffer than I was used to, but goddamn, he was right. It was like holding a pen, the way the brush slid over the canvas. I mean, it was just like sketching, except the color was so rich I couldn't believe it. A little later I said, "My god, what I've been missing."

"Yeah. Enjoy. I'll be back later."

He left me there with palette, brushes, paints, and canvas. I discovered texture, which I'd seen but never felt, and a universe opened to me that had been there all along.

We went down to the Arb that weekend, leaving about four in the morning, just like he said, to make sunrise, and we painted until sunset. We somehow made it home without driving into a ditch. I think the fact that he had a tape player in his car helped, but he had to pull over about half way and let me drive because he was falling asleep at the wheel. Now that I think of it, I still owe him for all the canvas I used.

2. *The Martyrdom of St. Bartholomew*

A painter *can* ignore nature, but he shouldn't. It isn't like architecture. An architect can't ignore nature, because if he doesn't pay attention to construction materials, the shape of the land, the climate, the soil, and all that, the house will fall down. (Of course, I can think of a few scandals with office buildings, but that's another issue.)

Just about any other kind of artist can fool himself into thinking that he's just looking at his own soul, as if it exists out in space somewhere.

I think every painter ought to study architecture. There is no better way to get a real understanding of space, and what will fit where, and a real feeling of displacing air. And there's more than that. I'm amazed by the number of things the architect has to take into account. The terrain, other buildings, what materials he has to work with and what the building will be used for. And furthermore, contriving a room so as to bring out a certain feeling in whoever steps into it, and simultaneously trying to express oneself through the overall shape and color of the exterior. It's like doing sculpture that has the additional feature of *inside*, and then has to be utilitarian as well.

When an architect talks about expressing what's in his soul, believe me, I'm going to listen. What was it Le Corbusier said? "Your mood has been gentle, brutal, charming or noble. The stones you have erected tell me so." And I've seen houses by Frank Lloyd Wright, and I've seen studies of Scarpa's Cimitero Brion, and the Museo di Castelvecchio. Yeah, I know that architects can use those lines and plans to express their souls. It can happen.

But what is in your soul is what was put there by everything you've ever done, or felt, or seen. What makes your painting work for other people is that the guy looking at your painting has also done, or felt, or seen, some of the same things. If you create art that is only playing off other art, like experimental jazz is playing off jazz, you're just pulling yourself further and further away from making any kind of meaningful statement.

So, on the one hand, to say, "I paint from nature," or, "I paint what I see," is silly, because you don't have any choice in the matter; of *course* that's what you're doing. The question is, how do you treat it? Are you trying to find what is common among you and all those who will see your work, or are you trying to separate yourself from the rest of the human race, desperate to be called, somehow, superior for this segregation?

On the other hand, if you spend all your time being introspective, trying as hard as you can to *deny* what you see, well, things are likely to come out pretty warped.

3. *The Adoration of the Golden Calf*

I walked in the studio door about two-thirty on Wednesday and discovered a full house. David was reading one of Parker's Spenser novels, Karen was talking to Bobby who was adding something yellow to the wall, and Dan, at the far end with his back to me, was looking at his painting. Scowling, presumably.

Mr. Winters was over, a short old guy with no chin and a few hundred wrinkles per square inch. When we started the place we found him in the want ads and hired him to clean the studio. This arrangement lasted almost a week, which was how long it took us to realize we couldn't afford him and that having someone in to clean up was courting disaster; if you don't know us you'd be hard pressed to tell what it is that matters around here and what's junk. We had to tell this to him, but he took it well and still drops by from time to time.

I loudly cleared my throat. "I suppose you're all wondering why I called you here today."

"Yawn," said David. Karen and Robert glanced at me, then went back to talking and painting, respectively.

Dan turned around, looking thoughtful. He said, "Actually—" It's always scary when Dan says that. "Since we *are* all here, we might as well talk." He came down the stairs and toward the front. I sighed and started grabbing folding chairs.

"Well, I'll be going then," said Mr. Winters. He

nodded to me. "You tell Debbie that I like that picture of the roses."

"I've told her," I said.

"I know. But tell her again."

I glanced at the photo, an eight and a half by eleven blow-up that I'd stuck to the wall near the door. It really was nice work—not everyone can make a black and white picture of roses work that well. I think Mr. Winters has a crush on Debbie.

He left as we finished setting up chairs.

"What do you want to talk about?" asked Robert of Dan, before I could.

"The show," said Dan. He sat down. So did the rest of us, except for David who just turned around and faced us, resting his arms on his spotless table. This put us in kind of a semi-circle around David, who seems to get off on his position. I think he just likes to show off how clean his area is. How can he get so much work done when nothing around him is ever out of place?

Karen "Broken Record" Schmidt said, "Can we afford it?"

"That's sort of the question, isn't it then?" said David in an almost-Liverpool accent.

"If we're going to rent a place, we'll have to rent it for a week. That'll run us about two hundred."

"What about using the studio?" asked David.

I moaned.

"I'd rather not," said Dan.

"Bless you, child," said I.

"For one thing, it would be almost impossible to keep working while we did. For another, it would be a lot of work to get it in shape; we'd have to cover over our walls, and that sort of thing. And for a third, who's going to come all the way over to this dump? You figure we're going to sell to the neighborhood?"

"Yeah, I guess," said David. "All right."

"Okay. We'll need flyers and stuff. We'll mail them out to anyone who's bought any of our work, or even come close to buying any of our work, and to all the galleries, and the Weekly and the Art Pages and the Dispatch and the art journals, and we'll have to tell the School of Art and design, and—"

"How much will that cost?" asked David.

"I don't know exactly. Call it a hundred and fifty for printing and mailing."

"Okay, that's three hundred and fifty."

"Opening day party supplies. Wine and cheese."

"Champagne," explained Robert.

Dan sighed. "I suppose."

Robert said, "What are we up to, Dan?"

"How much would supplies be? Three hundred? I don't know, with this and that, it would probably cost us about eight hundred by the time we finished."

"Eight hundred," I said. "That's all?" I was being sarcastic. "Any bright ideas on where we get it?"

"Take out a loan," said David. He got the appropriate giggles.

"I could take some calligraphy contracts," said Karen.

"Ouch," I said. "I'd rather we didn't have to start doing that. I mean, wasn't that the whole point of setting up the studio in the first place?"

"Well, yeah," she said. "But we aren't going to be able to much longer. Rent—"

"I know," I said.

"Look, guys," said David. "We might as well face the fact that it isn't working."

We just sat there for a while. In one sense, maybe we'd all been feeling that way, but it really caught me off guard to have it said like that. I mean, just, boom, there it is.

I finally said, "I'm not ready to give up," but I wasn't feeling anything like what I was saying.

Robert said, "That's the point of the show, isn't it? To make one more try? We've tried all the galleries, applied for all the grants, so, you know, I think it's worth taking one more shot at it."

I hadn't looked at it that way, and, from the expressions around the room, I guess the others hadn't either. Karen was nodding. "I can see that," she said. "But it doesn't answer the question: How are we going to raise eight hundred dollars?"

After a moment, Dan said, "Let's just think about it, okay?"

"I bet we could figure out a way," said Robert.

I wasn't so confident, but there was a glimmer of anticipation starting, way down deep somewhere. I do wonder what it was from. Maybe just that anticipation you always get when something is about to change; even if the change is for the worse, the anticipation can be there. I mean, I didn't want to get a job as a draftsman, but I could, and there was something to be said for a steady income, and not making Debbie support me any more. In fact, the more I thought about it, the nicer it sounded. The idea of not worrying about next month's rent had a certain appeal to it. And if the show worked out, well, all to the good.

I said, "What we really need is to make sure the papers or somebody covers the show. There are plenty of people around who are willing to look at something different, and who can afford to buy it if they like it. If they heard of us—"

"Okay," said David. "How do we do it? We don't really have any connections, do we?"

"Not around here," said Robert. "Want to move to New York?"

Karen said, "Who do you know in New York?"

"No one," said Robert, "but with so much to choose from, we're bound to meet somebody eventually."

I couldn't figure out if he was joking or not. I decided not to ask. That seemed to be about all there was to say, though, so people started standing up. I hung around. Pretty soon it was David and me sitting there.

He said, "The thing is, I just can't really conceive of anyone spending money for my work. It isn't that I don't think it's any good, it's just, I don't know, I can't really imagine it."

I didn't say anything because I knew exactly how he felt. I stood up and got back to work.

4. *Charles I and Henrietta Maria
with the Liberal Arts*

I was inspired, that day.

Maybe it was talking about the show that did it, I don't know; but I picked up a brush, and, almost at once, I knew exactly what I was doing.

I needed a whole. I needed to communicate a theme, to get across what the whole painting was about. Uranus was dying at the hands of Artemis and Apollo—but why? Was this to be a senseless killing? Why were they doing it? What need could cause divine beings to take the life of another divine being? What need can cause a human being to take the life of another?

Most of the answers to that led me to an Artemis and an Apollo that I wouldn't have wanted to paint. But, no, these were *gods*. This was an act of *creation*. Creation embodied in destruction? Nothing so simple, I decided. I'd played with that idea before. No, this would be an act of release.

The whole painting would center upon Artemis and Uranus, with Apollo subservient to Artemis, and the expressions on their faces, and the background. I needed to show the world opening up, and...

A gateway, that's what I saw. There needed to be the

movement toward a gate, with Uranus blocking the path no longer.

The colors were mixed, the tint was built, the brush-strokes went on, short and choppy at first, then languorous, then thick gobs building toward the gate, which was foreboding yet intriguing; the center of the action but off to the side of the painting, part of it, in fact, vanishing out of the canvas. I wanted the viewer to want to see beyond it, yet it would always draw his eye in to Artemis and Uranus.

I didn't step back to look at how I was doing, because I could *feel* it happening. In one sense, no, I didn't know if it would be any good, but I knew it was what I had to do then, and forcing myself to slow down and study each stroke would have been impossible.

Later, as I worked hard and fast and furiously, I wondered whether this was going to be too pat, too easy, too much the formula or the heavy-handed symbolism. But I couldn't worry about that now.

The madness was upon me and I gloried in it.

5. *The Fortune Teller*

Csucskári followed the cave, which was long and dark. It went up and down, and twisted from side to side so that he was afraid he would become lost. But suddenly he knew what he could do, and he made a light spring up around him. It came none too soon, either, because he had been about to fall into a pit.

With the light around him, he soon comes to a place where the sow is nursing her nine piglets. Before you could say, *palacsinták*, he takes out his jackknife and slits open her belly. Inside, he finds a box. He holds it up to his ear, and he hears the twelve wasps buzzing around inside. He puts the box into his pocket, then he starts to leave.

The sow says, "Come, Csucskári, didn't my husband the boar ask you to sew me back up, so I may feed my nine piglets?"

"Well, yes he did," says Csucskári. "Since you have reminded me of it, I will do so." Csucskári found a spider's web, and from it he made a length of thread, and with a bee's stinger he made a needle. With these he quickly sewed up the wound in the sow's belly.

When he had finished, the sow said, "You have been faithful and sewed up my belly, so I will tell you something."

Csucskári said, "What is it you will tell me then?"

The sow says, "You should know that there is a dragon with twelve heads, a dragon with ten heads, and a dragon with eight heads, and you will have to fight them all if you wish to set the sun, the moon, and the stars up in the sky."

"Well, mother," says Csucskári, "it is good of you to tell me this. How will I find these dragons?" You see, he was determined to meet them head on.

The sow said, "You must continue through the cave, not going back the way you came, and you will soon be on a path, and then you will see a cottage where lives the dragon with twelve heads. No more can I tell you."

"Then thank you, and may you live a long time and have many children."

With these words, Csucskári set off through the cave, still surrounded by his own light, until he emerged at last onto a path. He took the path, and soon saw a small cottage, and as he approached it his light went out.

6. *The Laughing Cavalier*

I never really know what I'm doing, and that's because, maybe, I always know what I'm doing too well.

I made a big thing about starting out a painting without having any idea where I'm going. But I'd love to see what would happen to an architect who just started in designing and see where it took him, without paying attention to whether he was creating an office complex, a house, or a parking ramp. It probably wouldn't work.

And I'll tell you, because I can't tell anyone else, that sometimes when I think I'm just starting in to see where the brush takes me, I don't really know if that's what I'm doing at all. Maybe I'm fooling myself, and those "discoveries" are coldly planned by a coldly planning part of me that lies somewhere between the conscious and the subconscious, and it is the conceit of this part of my ego that wants to make an *artistic* parking ramp, because it knows that a parking ramp is all it's capable of.

People need parking ramps, too, though; don't they?

So why do I find the thought so upsetting?

Bones?

CHAPTER
•SEVEN•

1. PEASANTS PLAYING SHUFFLEBOARD

TIMING HAS ALWAYS been a particular skill of mine.

For instance, I managed to quit school just when I was about done with the most boring art classes and was ready to start on the interesting ones. I still don't know why I quit. Maybe I was having so much fun painting that I was sure I couldn't earn a living at it.

I wasn't wrong about that, either, but so what? If I was going to try to do it, I should have stuck with school.

I suppose it didn't help that none of the profs thought my work was "interesting."

Shit. "Interesting." I *hate* that word. It's got to be the biggest one-word excuse for bad art there is. "He did something really interesting with line," they say. What I hear is, "He was masturbating with a paint brush." The last grant I applied for went to someone who was creating art with ant farms. I'm not kidding. Ant farms. I can well believe the results were "interesting."

Can I tell you a story? When I was a kid, I was in Chicago with my father, and we stopped by the John Hancock Center, where they have this huge "sculpture" (for lack of a better word) by Picasso, for which Chicago paid him a couple of million or something. My father studied it for a while then asked a nearby guard, "What do you think Picasso was saying with this sculpture?"

The guard said, "I think he was saying, 'Ha, ha, Chicago.' "

Yeah. I think he was right.

But that's off the subject.

For whatever reason, I quit the "U" and went to a vo-tech to learn drafting at the beginning of what would have been my junior year.

I hated it, but I have a piece of paper that could probably get me a job if I had to. Good draftsmen aren't all that easy to find. If drafting jobs were a little harder to come by, I wouldn't be so tempted, and if I weren't so tempted, I might be happier.

Or maybe just more desperate.

2. *The Cemetery*

About a year ago Debbie and I went to see a film by Szabo. All the way home she was bubbling about the cinematography. We'd argued about this before, and I resolved not to say anything. By the time we got home, I couldn't stand it any more. I grunted, "I liked it."

She stared at me. "Just what's your problem this time?"

"Same thing," I said. "The point of a motion picture is motion. If I want to see theater, we can see a play."

"You're saying—"

"I'm tired of nonsense dialogue said by people contorting their faces into revolting expressions to follow the machinations of a hackneyed plot."

She stared at me. "You think—"

"Well, no, it wasn't really that bad. It's just it misses the point of movies. It's *motion, movement.*"

"I don't see what you're after, Greg."

"I want to see an artist with a camera. That's all. I've never seen one. Christ! Can you imagine what Millet would have done with motion pictures?"

"No, and I don't especially want to."

"Well, he wouldn't have turned it into theater on film, that's for sure. He'd have found a peasant picking wheat, and shown it for thirty seconds, and produced more beauty and more human emotion than—"

"How can an artist be so blind to art?" she said.

I shrugged and we stopped arguing about it. But that question has stayed with me.

I mean, what if she's right?

3. *The Triumph of the Name of Jesus*

I got in late Thursday, after the advanced sparring class. We'd been working on tai sabaki, which is one of my favorite things to work on, and maybe someday I'll actually be able to use it. I'd had the dubious pleasure of sparring with Peter, so I knew I'd hurt tomorrow, but I'd enjoyed it. I came in fired up with energy, my feet dancing. Robert was staring over David's shoulder near the door. I said, "Hiya, Unca Bobby," and roundhouse kicked his beret off his head. He turned around, annoyed.

"Don't do that, all right? I mean it."

"Sorry," I said, and I was. "I'm just feeling hyper."

"Well, feel hyper at your painting or something."

David gestured to his sketch and said, "What d'ya think?"

I looked at what he'd done, and felt my pulse quicken. "Yeah!" I said. "I like it! Shit man, that's really nice."

He looked relieved, which was quite gratifying. "Should I put in more background?"

"Hell, no," I said.

"I don't know," said Robert. He pointed to the big white area in the upper left. "There ought to be *something* here, I think. Just to bring your eye into the face more."

"No way," I said. "The eyes do that all by themselves. And I really like the way you rendered her hair."

He nodded. "I'll ask Karen and Dan when they show up."

"Karen won't be in," said Robert. "She's at home putting a portfolio together."

"To do what with?" I asked.

"She wants to go around to some galleries."

"Heh. I wish her luck."

"So do I," said Robert. "I mean it."

I looked at him. "Is something bothering you?"

He shrugged. "I think you have an attitude problem."

"Attitude problem," I said. "Attitude problem."

"Yeah."

"You talking about Karen?"

"Yeah."

"Why? Because I don't fall all over myself every time she picks up a brush?"

"To be honest," put in David. "I don't think she's all that great either."

Robert said, "Okay, but you don't take every chance you can find to cut her down behind her back, either."

I said, "I'm not cutting *her* down; just her work," which may be one of history's most transparent lies.

Robert shrugged, screwed his face up, and looked away. I studied him for a moment, then said, "Hey, Unca Bobby. You got something going with her?"

He turned back. "Why do you say that?"

"If I wanted to paint you right now, I'd call it, 'Young Man in Love.'"

That got a smile from him. He said, "Could be."

I said, "Yeah, well, I'll lighten up a little."

He said, "It would be worth more if you'd work with her; give some useful suggestions once in a while."

I had to think about that. Finally I said, "Okay, I know that I'm not all that impressed with what she's doing, but how do I know I'm right? Why should I push her into doing something she doesn't want to do, if I might be wrong?"

"You aren't bashful about telling David or me what to fix."

I swallowed and rephrased that in my mind so I wouldn't take it wrong and make things worse. Then I said, as slowly and carefully as I could, "I *like* what you and David do. I try to make suggestions that will help you get an effect you're after. I assume that's what you guys do with me. It's a different thing."

"No it isn't," put in David. "When we started we said we'd help each other; that doesn't mean just with the nit picks. If you think she needs to do different subjects, or take a whole different approach, you ought to tell her so. So should I, I guess. It's the same thing."

Robert said, "We all respected each other's work when we started. That was the point, wasn't it?"

"Yeah, well you guys and Dan have *grown*. She hasn't. She's doing the same things now she was when we started, only maybe a little slicker."

"I don't agree," said Robert. "But if I did, I'd tell her so."

"Maybe," I said.

"Not maybe," said Robert.

"Okay, I'll think about it."

"You know what I think?" said Robert. "I think she's likely to sell before any of the rest of us. I think she does work that reaches people—that says something to them."

"That," I said, "is unlikely. Her paintings don't say anything to me."

Robert said, "Has it occurred to you to wonder why it is that the only one of us you're contemptuous of is the one woman in the group?"

"Oh, God, spare me."

"Well, has it?"

"Yeah, Rob, as a matter of fact, it has. I've thought about it, and I don't buy it." Robert shrugged. I looked over to David, hoping for support, but he was chewing his lip and looking down. I said, "It's like a witch-hunt, you know? All you have to do is accuse someone of being sexist, and it's like he's tainted. You don't have to prove—"

"Oh, God, spare me," said Robert.

I suddenly wanted very badly to hit him.

I wanted to badly enough that I had to force myself to stand still and take a couple of deep breaths. We stood there like that, and I had to wonder if I'd have gotten so mad if there weren't some truth in what he said.

"Fuck," I announced, and turned away.

I walked over to my area. I wondered if Robert would still be pissed at me when he got around to looking at my painting, and, if he was, whether it would carry over. That was a scary thought. If he was going to let that sort of thing influence what he said, I couldn't listen to him.

Would he really do that?

Would *I* do that?

I hoped not; I'd try not to. But would I be able to prevent it? If I were really pissed at, say, David, would I be able to be objective about his work? I'd have to say what it made me feel, and explain where I was coming from so he could take it into account. That would be a real ugly situation.

I looked up and saw the Monster staring at me. I stared back, seeing something. I said, "Shit. I hadn't noticed that before," and got to work.

4. *The Immaculate Conception*

The first figure to emerge, Uranus, was just to the left of the middle. Artemis balanced it on the other side by being almost as close to the center and almost as big, with the line of his arm continuing the line of the mountain in toward Artemis, who was looking at Uranus.

All well and good, but when I'd put in the gate in the upper left, it had thrown the balance off, especially since it was so bright. The gate was too eye-catching to match the mountain, which was what it ought to have done.

You understand, "balance" isn't a mechanical thing, like everything has to exactly match and even out, but on the other hand, you ought to have some kind of balance centered on the point that catches the eye.

Shit. I should have sketched it first.

I studied it for a long time—long enough for some of the flaws to start bothering me, and I knew I'd have to go back and clean some of them up before I did much more. But, no, it just didn't work—the balance was off. I have nothing against making the viewer uncomfortable (I, at least, don't find Van Gogh's "Sorrow" to be especially soothing), but there has to be a reason, and for this one, the *balance* had to be comfortable so the *theme* would make you think. The contrast between them was what the painting was all about.

I hadn't realized that before.

I shook off the meditations. Okay, Greg: Think. I didn't want to mess with the mountains, they were just right. The main figures had some problems (I was going to have to fix Apollo's ear, for instance), but they were generally right, and I didn't want to try to move them anyway. Cropping was right out; I know some painters do it, but I say it's spinach and I say to hell with it.

I could mess with the gate. I studied it, and realized that if I changed it at all, it would be to call *more* attention to it—maybe I'd gloss it a bit, to assert a similarity to Apollo.

Another figure? What? Where?

Behind Apollo (just to the left) was an interesting grayish swirl that I hadn't done anything with. Could I put something there without cluttering up the work? It was big enough so I *should* be able to.

I stared at it again, startled. Now how the hell had I gotten that color? What a weird, interesting gray. It was dark, especially in contrast to the way Apollo was shining nearby, and shot with dark blue highlights, and just a little trace of yellow.

I put the colors out on the palette and started mixing, testing it on random pieces of canvas that I keep on my table. I stopped from time to time to hold the test next to the original, and, sometime in there I started getting excited. Why does an interesting color excite me so much? I mixed the colors faster, and I barely noticed when I started having trouble finding the pure colors on my palette.

Sometime in there, I'm not sure when, I started working on the canvas itself, then I became a part of it and fell into it, creating the world around me with my brush, brain dead, disconnected; the vegetables danced at the teddy bears' picnic with the Wolfe howling like an electric Kesey cookoo test, and eventually achieved a balance of Dionysian frenzy with sedate cognition, and it moved me, brightly.

I painted myself out of a corner, but I wasn't there so I can't take the credit.

5. *Skittle Players Outside an Inn*

Csucskári stood outside the house and looked at it for a long time (he was waiting for the dragon, you know). He went closer and closer, but didn't see any dragon. Finally, he goes inside. He sees a woman there. She says, "Ah, you are Csucskári!"

"Well, yes I am," says Csucskári.

The woman says, "When you were smaller than a hundredth part of a grain in your mother's womb, I knew my husband would kill you."

"Oh, you don't need to worry about that," says Csucskári. "Is your husband a dragon?"

"A dragon!" cries the woman. "Why, he is a dragon with twelve heads!"

"That's all right then," says Csucskári. (He wasn't frightened.) "Only tell me, is there a sign of his coming?"

"Yes there is," said the woman. "When he is twelve miles away, he grips his mace, which weighs twelve hundred pounds, and hurls it with such force that it makes the cornerstones crack."

Csucskári went outside, and saw that the mace had already arrived and made the cornerstones crack. He picked up the mace and started walking. Then he threw it with such force that it traveled more than twelve miles back the way it had come.

Soon he came to a field, and in the field was a ditch, and over the ditch was a bridge. He went down into the ditch and picked up a big rock and broke it over his knee.

Then he broke it again and again until it looked like a sword, and this he sharpened with his teeth. Then he thrust the sword through the cracks of the bridge.

Well, pretty soon along comes the dragon on his horse. First thing you know, the horse trips over the sword and the dragon falls down on the bridge.

"What is this?" cries the dragon to his horse. "May your blood be lapped up by dogs! Haven't you done twelve good miles this day without as much as a false step? I guess it's Csucskári who is playing a nasty trick on us. If I knew for sure, I'd make him pay with his head."

When Csucskári heard these words, he was so mad that his anger melted the rock he was standing on, and he jumped up onto the bridge.

"Ho, my twelve-headed friend!" he cries. "You want my head? I'd like to know what you wish to do with it, since you have twelve of your own, and not a brain in any of them. A poor reward, I'd call it, for all the trouble I'm taking to fix the sun and the moon in the sky so that we may live in light instead of darkness."

Says the dragon with twelve heads, "Never mind about that now. You'd better tell me how you want to fight me. Is it to be the sword, or shall we measure each other's strength in a fist fight?"

Now, Csucskári is still pretty mad about what the dragon had said, so he says, "It is neither by the sword nor in a fist fight that we are going to settle this. My father was neither a cattle driver nor a cowherd, so why should I bother about your challenge?"

Then he stepped up and, with two strokes, cut off all twelve of the dragon's heads. Then he went on his way again, off down the road.

6. *A Woman Bathing in a Stream*

What many people don't seem to realize is that "technically competent" and "detailed" do not automatically add up to "good." What many critics don't realize is that "interesting" is no more than it says.

The idea isn't to show off how much detail you can capture, the idea is to use exactly the *right* details to express what you want to express, and no more. Which isn't to say that every painting with a lot of detail is overdone, either. Gericault often used incredible amounts of tiny detail, but he was a genius. Cezanne used very little, and he was a genius, too. Did you know that there are around twenty-four hundred different kinds of crickets? Okay, now you tell me: how many pictures are you going to paint where it matters whether the thing at the bottom is an Australian Grey or a tree cricket? Hell, how many pictures are you going to paint where anything matters except that it's a *bug?*

You need to be technically skilled enough to do anything, but then you have to know when not to.

And as to the critics: how can you get excited about something, and then explain that you're so excited because it's "interesting?" Interesting means there is something there that catches your interest, and that's great. A painting ought to catch your interest. A trap that catches a mouse is a very useful thing, and I'm glad they exist. But I'll get excited when I see a trap that catches a hippo.

Do you know *why* they are so excited because something is interesting? Because they're bloody well *jaded,* that's why. They've seen it all before. They're tired of it, and they want something new, different, *interesting.*

Well, that's fine, but just because the critics are jaded doesn't mean the human race is jaded. So, yes, a work of art ought to be "interesting," but that's just the start. It has to evoke human emotion.

I don't mean to suggest that evoking emotion is enough. Landseer's "The Old Shepherd's Chief Mourner" is considered a masterpiece, but to me it's just saccharine. But I can respect what he was after, nevertheless. He wanted people to feel pity for a lonely old man, and he wanted to do it without ever showing the old man. Millet was after a similar feeling in, say, "The Angelus," and he got it. But so many artists today don't have time for that; they're too interested in creating something "interesting," in the "conceptual edge," to waste time with something as pedestrian as pity.

But where else can it come from? If not in art, where is there room for sharing the hurts of the world, and spreading them out a little and so take some of the sting away? If an artist can't do it, no one can.

If an artist can't do it, he's no artist.

Bones?

CHAPTER
•EIGHT•

1. *THE INQUISITION*

I DON'T KNOW how I did so well in drafting school since I had no interest in it at all. But then, I've always been good at sanding pencil tips.

We were graded on things like ends of lines meeting, and evenness of line, et boring cetera. By the time we got to some of the computer stuff (which was fun), I knew I'd be miserable doing that sort of thing eight hours a day. I rushed through the assignments, then used the school supplies to do sketches of fellow students when they weren't looking.

One of them caught me at it, because he'd been doing the same thing, which was how I got to know Robert.

I'm not sure how we'd missed meeting up to that point, which was about halfway through the nine month course. He, like me, drove a Jap cycle, and we wore the same kind of leather jackets (thank you Berman Buckskin), and we were both near the top of the class. This latter was something the school made no secret of, which is why I don't want to tell you which school it was; I don't believe in that.

We started hanging out together, hitting The Revue, which had just changed its name and was starting to have good music. We started competing with each other doing drawings—and cartoons and caricatures—of fellow students. I mentioned painting, but he didn't seem interested. He brought in some pen and ink stuff and I said, "Been to Japan lately?"

He said, "Dig it." He hadn't really been there. The Art Institute had had a showing of Japanese prints and he had been working that way ever since. He had some really fine stuff.

I was still in touch with David, so the three of us got together and sat up all night arguing artists (am I the only guy in the world who likes Girodet?) and enjoyed it so much that we did it again—the second time without drugs. Eventually David introduced us to Dan and Karen, whom he'd gotten to know while I was at tech school, and pretty soon we were showing each other our work.

One day when I was out drinking with David, he said, out of nowhere, "How well do you know Robert?"

I shrugged. "Pretty well, I guess."

"Is he honest?"

"He overbids at bridge."

David blinked. "He plays bridge?"

"Yeah."

"How good is he?"

"Not bad. He overbids, though."

"That settles it, then. He's in."

"In what?"

"Dan and Karen and I have been talking about trying to set up a studio when we graduate. We were wondering if you and Robert might be interested."

The five of us spent a few weeks talking about it in more and more detail. I had saved some bucks, so I could hold my end up, and I didn't ask the others any embarrassing questions, and we were all graduating at the same time, so we finally said, what the hell? We decided to try it for a couple of years.

That was three years ago. It's been good. I don't know how much longer we can last.

2. *Bathsheba*

When I think of Renaissance painting I don't think of oil on canvas. There was some of that, of course, but for the most part, it was tempera on the walls of churches, in large frescoes and panels. The subject matter wasn't always religious, but it usually was.

After that came large canvases when you were painting for the King or the Emperor, and the subjects were from Greek mythology, or, again, religious work. They got into smaller canvases when they were painting for the burgher and the Dutch merchant who wanted something in his living room. What he wanted in his living room was what he saw every day; the street scene, the maiden, portraits of himself and his family, and maybe an occasional still-life or landscape to relax him.

We're going backward, in a way. The wall of our studio, and what we did with it, isn't something that was original with us. All over the Little Town area near the "U" there are buildings decorated and painted, usually with easy political slogans—the religious work of today on today's panels and churches (usually grocery stores).

And in New York is the highest expression of abstractionist art—the stuff being done with spray paint on a subway car. Today's vandalism; tomorrow's masterpiece. We weren't aware of what we were doing when we started playing with the walls of the studio, we were just having a good time. That says something, too. It all comes around, I guess.

3. *Tobias and the Angel*

There were fireworks when I came in after training on Friday. Dan and Robert, of all unlikely combinations, were really going at it, facing each other across Robert's table, where he had a bunch of studies of faces from a nursing home near his apartment. I could tell right away it was something serious; Robert was waving his finger at Dan and saying, "So, now you gonna get an airbrush, too?"

Dan said, "I hadn't planned on it."

Robert went on, "When we started, we said, 'no compromises,' right?"

"When we started we were idiots," said Dan.

"Maybe, but that's what we said, right?"

"We said no compromises for two years. It's been almost three."

"So, does that mean we're dead? Is the great experiment over?"

"It means that you're making a big deal out of nothing."

"I don't think it's nothing. That's the whole point. Once you start—"

"Start what?" I put in.

They turned and looked at me, then they both started speaking at once, stopped, started again, then Dan shut up. Robert said, "Dan wants us—"

"Me," said Dan. "I didn't say anything about the rest of you."

Robert brushed that off like a fly on his jacket. "Dan wants to start doing advertising art."

You know the expression, "He looked like his teeth hurt?" Well, I think I felt what must go with that look. But I finally said, "Robert, if he needs the money—"

"That's the point. He doesn't need the fucking money, he wants to do it so we can do the show."

I said, "Jesus, Dan, is that true? What's the point?"

"The point is, if we can't do the show, or something, we're going straight down the tubes."

"All right then," said Robert, "we go down the tubes. At least we can do it honestly."

Seeing no reason to confine myself to only one side of the argument, I said, "Rob, do you really think one or two freelance jobs are going to—"

"You're goddamn right I do. Especially if Dan does them. It takes him ten years to do a painting anyway. Does he want to spend all his time doing layouts or something?"

"As opposed to what?" snapped Dan. "Have you seen them lining up outside to buy the work I've done so far?" Ah! I thought. Now we come to it. "So, I've got all these paintings. Who's going to buy them?"

I said, "There are art lovers out there, Dan. We just have to let them know we're here."

"Right," he said. "That's why we want to do the show. And we can't do that without some bucks. That's just how it is."

Just how it is.

I walked over to look at "Lost." God, but it was lovely. I don't know how he does it. I felt tears starting, and there was an honest-to-god lump in my throat. Where did he get his genius? Was it, like, a well that I could drink from, too? I shrugged it aside. It comes from the same place any inspired art comes from, I mused. I just wish I could tap into it. I sighed and looked again at the canvas. *He* was going to start doing advertising? No. That was wrong. It was just *wrong*.

I walked back to where the two of them were still going at it, and interrupted. I said, "Look, Dan, will you give it a little more time before you make a decision?"

He studied me as if he were trying to read my mind. "How long?" he asked after a moment.

"Not long. A couple, three weeks maybe?"

"What do you have in mind?"

"I just want to see if something is going to break, okay?"

There was another pause, then he said, "Yeah, okay. A couple, three weeks."

"Thanks," I said. "I need to get some air."

I went back downstairs, not stopping to look at the Monster. I sat down on David's table and tried to put the whole thing out of my mind. What jumped in its place was the whole ugly mess with Karen. I sighed. I tried to imagine myself walking up to her and saying, "Karen, you should know that I really don't respect you as an artist." I couldn't picture it. Just as well.

Was Robert right, though? Shit. The curse of the middle-class white male in the 80's. Oh, woe is me, am I sexist? Am I racist?

What a load of crap.

I walked over and took another look at her bird and snake. It was nice. But it was *empty*. Try as hard as I could, I couldn't make it pull any emotion from me. I wondered what Dan would do with the subject, but that was pointless. Think about something else, Greg.

Which brought me back to the Monster, which I didn't want to think about either. Which brought me back to Deb, and our living arrangements, which wasn't any more pleasant. Which brought me back to the show.

I glanced up and saw that Robert was looking at me. I put on a smile, and stood up suddenly, trying to put some cheerful bounce in my movements, waved, and walked out the door.

When I came back an hour later I was full of coffee from Bill and Toni's. Under my jacket I hid the morning paper folded to the want ads. There had been three ads for draftsmen.

I walked back to my area, grateful for the screens, and started painting right away.

4. *Esther Before Ahasuerus*

I was too involved by this time to have any feel for the whole. I knew this stage, too—it's where self-doubt comes and sits on my shoulder like a vulture. It's not unreasonable self-doubt, either, because I've done a lot of bad work, and I get too close to it to tell.

It didn't help that no one had looked at it in close to a week—since right after I'd started. But that was my own fault. Usually I want the others—especially David and Dan—to tell me what they think as I go. But I was too involved in this painting, and I knew that even if they said, "Forget it, it stinks," I'd have to keep going. And, moreover, they would *certainly* find problems, even if they liked it in general, and then I'd have to go back and fix them, and I didn't want to do that just then. I wanted to paint, and paint, and finish it. I *had* to finish it. I'd never felt such a driving need before.

It was so clear in my mind, too. I wanted Artemis to be so real you could touch her, and to be jumping out of the canvas, and for Uranus to be so flat against it he was almost part of the canvas itself, and the light from Apollo to dissipate throughout the whole, as if Apollo were the light source for the painting.

I put in a few shadows to enhance this effect, then

realized that I hadn't really dealt with shadowing for any of it at all. Well, that would be today's project: Shadows. I really could do the whole thing as if Apollo were the light source, but I'd have to be very careful not to make it too obvious. I mean, I didn't have any particular symbolism in mind for that, and I know that if you put too much emphasis on something it becomes a symbol, and if you put a little more it becomes an obvious, cheap, sleazy symbol.

I worked very carefully, using only touches of color, which was red mixed with a bit of black, and I suggested shadows everywhere except around Apollo. It would be there if you looked close.

I sighed and stepped back, wondering if the whole thing was getting too cluttered. The wolf I had added to the foreground might look like a cheap symbol, too, now that I thought of it. Well, if it did, Dan and David would tell me. But, dammit, I needed the balance.

I thought about going back and cleaning up some of the ground—washing it out, as it were, to produce a more stark effect.

I discovered that I was standing there, unable to decide, for longer than I ought to, so I cleaned my brushes and palette and packed it in. I needed to get home early, anyway, and start working on my resume. It would be too depressing to do it over the weekend.

5. The Stonemason's Yard

Csucskári was tired after the battle with the dragon with twelve heads, so he set off down the road looking for a place to rest. Soon, he comes to a house. He goes inside and says, "Hello, woman," to the woman who is there.

"Well, good day to you, Csucskári," she says (she recognizes him).

"How is it you know me, woman?" asked Csucskári.

The woman said, "When you were smaller than the hundredth part of a grain in your mother's womb, I knew that my husband, the dragon with ten heads, would fight you because you killed his brother."

"Ah," said Csucskári. "So this is the home of the dragon with ten heads? Well, I had hoped for a bit of rest after fighting his brother, but I can see I have more work to do. So you tell me then, what is the sign of his coming?"

"When he gets within ten miles of his house, he grips his mace, which weighs a thousand pounds, and hurls it at this castle with such force that the weathercock on the top of the roof will make an about-face."

So Csucskári stepped out of the house, and, just as he did, it all happened as the woman had predicted. As quick as you please, Csucskári went and hid in a nearby ditch spanned by a bridge, just as before. Again, he thrust his sword through the boards. When the dragon came riding up the bridge, his horse suddenly tripped over the sword.

"Ho!" cried the dragon. "May your blood be lapped up by dogs. What's that? Haven't you done ten good miles this day without as much as a false step? I know this is all Csucskári's doing. To be sure I'll make him pay for it. He killed my brother, the dragon with twelve heads, and I'll take his life for it."

When Csucskári heard this kind of talk, all thoughts of rest were gone and he leapt up onto the bridge. "Come on, comrade, let's see whether your fighting is as good as your words."

At that they rushed at one another. All the clock round they were dealing each other blows with the flats of their swords, and they made such a tumult that all of the grain was swept out of the fields and into bins, yet they continued.

Another day went by, and they tried each other with

the points of their swords, but neither could gain the advantage; each was the equal of the other, yet they kicked up such a fuss that all the hay was struck down and baled and put into the barns.

On the third day, Csucskári at last brought the fight to a close by dealing a blow with his sword, cutting off all ten of the dragon's heads at one mighty sweep.

Then he set off down the road, looking for a place to rest.

6. *The Piazza Navona Flooded*

What you have to remember when looking at a painting is this: nothing is accidental. Maybe that seems obvious, and maybe it seems trivial, but it isn't either one. If something is emphasized, the artist wanted it emphasized. If something is played down, the artist wanted it played down. Even more, if there is a wisp of a bird off in one corner of the landscape, that bird is there for a reason.

If the artist was Rossetti, the bird symbolizes freedom. If it was Monet, he needed the splash of color. If it was Gericault, he wanted movement in an otherwise still scene. If it was Audubon, that's the subject of the painting. If it was Thoma, he happened to see a bird there when he looked.

It takes an effort, an act of will, and physical movement of a physical brush with paint on it, to put in that bird, whether you're James Whistler and you spend six years on a wing, or you're Van Gogh and suggest "bird" with one plunge of brush to canvas. It's there because the artist wanted it.

I don't always know exactly *why* I want something to be in the painting, or why I want it a certain way. Sometimes I do, but sometimes it just feels right. Then I have the pleasure of figuring out why just as you do, after it's done.

Sometimes it isn't a pleasure—I decide it was a mistake. But usually, by that time, it's too late to change it. I could spend my life repainting mistakes I made that are so small I can't describe them but so big I can't miss them.

Sometimes the whole piece is a mistake from the beginning, but I can't know that, either, until it's done, and then, as before, it's too late.

Timing, that's what it is.

Bones?

CHAPTER
• NINE •

1. *A SPORTING CONTEST ON THE RIVER TIBER*

WHEN I WAS about twelve, I went to Hungary with my father. We spent about a week bicycling up and down the streets and hills of Budapest. When I think of that time, images and feelings flash before my mind like a slide show done with strobe lights — the food, the faces, the museums, the buildings.

At one point we visited the Temple of Saint Istvan — the patron saint of Hungary. I remember it as a grand, massive cube on top of a hill. In front was a statue of a

Russian soldier, erected, I guess, by a grateful populace
after World War II. On the other side was a wall riddled
with machine gun bullets from 1956. As if that weren't
enough of a statement, the government representatives
were outside the door, handing out crucifixes to all and
sundry. We didn't take one.

Inside it was gorgeous and huge. My senses were
numbed almost at once, so there are few details I can call
up, yet I remember niches in the wall holding exhibits,
and I remember the grace and simple beauty of the fur-
nishings, that now recall to me Japanese pottery in their
unpretentious elegance.

There was a traditional peasant wedding going on in
the center of the cathedral with, I seem to recall, several
hundred participants. We were in the same "room," along
with, maybe, a thousand other visitors, yet there was no
contact between the groups. That's what I remember
about the size.

We had almost completed the circuit of the cathedral
when we arrived below a large, ornate plaque, with, I
think, black raised lettering against a grayish background.
It was probably of wrought iron. I asked my father what
it said and he told me.

"No, Dad," I said. "In English."

So he translated it. It was something about how we
are all little lambs of Jesus. I nodded soberly and we
moved on. Then my father came up behind me and sang
very softly in my ear:

"I am Jesus' little lamb,
    Yes, you're God damn right I am."

I cracked up, of course. Hysterical laughter, right
there in the midst of everything. I couldn't stop. People
started looking at me. I tried to pretend I was having an
attack of coughing; you know, cough cough laugh laugh
cough cough.

No good.

Up comes the bouncer.

She looked to be about ninety. She started rattling off to me in Hungarian and pointing to the exit. I was afraid that in another minute she might become violent.

I went up to my father, who had his hands clasped behind his back and was carefully looking the other way.

"Dad," I said. "She wants us to leave."

"Well," he said, without looking around. "I guess you'd better leave, then."

I had a moment of shocked disbelief, then I allowed the bouncer to escort me out of the place. I sat there, fuming, on the cement retaining wall across the way from the entrance, below the noble Russian soldier.

My father emerged about five minutes later, looking thoughtful. I was prepared to tear into him, but before I could open my mouth he said, "You know, Greg, you'll never get anywhere with people by laughing at their beliefs."

That's Hungary, that's the temple of Saint Istvan, and that's my father.

2. *Cleopatra Before Octavius*

Remember what I said before about art critics being so bored with art that they need something interesting to excite them? Well, a friend of mine named David (different David; you haven't met him) once said the same about poetry. The similarities to painting are obvious — the importance of rhythm and texture, the relationship of form to subject, and the fact that what seems to be popular among critics is work that few people have any interest in.

You know what poetry excites me? Song lyrics. Good ones, that is — there's an excess of trash there, too. But in terms of moving you with the imagery, the sound and the beauty of the words, and depth of content, I'll take Dylan,

or Paul Simon on a good day, or Robert Hunter, or
Springsteen's early stuff. Yet song lyrics are as disdained
by literary critics as illustration is by the art world.

You know, now that I think of it, I wouldn't mind
being the Bob Dylan of painting. That wouldn't bother
me at all.

3. Croesus Sacrificing Himself to save Callirrhoe

Robert has always hung out with the kind of people
whom one doesn't ask, "Are you on drugs?" One just
assumes the person is and can deal with whatever comes
up. I don't think he uses much himself anymore. I asked
him once if he ever worked while high and he said,
"Yeah. Groove on the colors, man," which was especially
nice since he does nothing except pen and ink.

I stopped working when I heard the door open Saturday evening. I ducked my head out past the screens, saw
Robert, put my stuff down and came out.

He looked stoned. Not drunk — he was walking fine.
Not what I'd call high — he seemed to be seeing the same
things I was. But I would have guessed he was stoned out
of his mind. His face was slack, his expression projected
vagueness like a Morandi still life. His eyelids were
drooping, and his whole body seemed limp.

I said, "You all right, Rob?"

He said, "Huh? Yeah, I'm fine, I guess."

"You guess?"

"Huh? Yeah, I'm fine."

There was a second or two while I stood there, trying
to decide what to do, then I shrugged and went back and
painted some more. After a while I realized that there
were no sounds coming from the rest of the room — I
couldn't even hear Robert breathing. That spooked me a
little, so I put the brushes down and went out.

He was over by his table, just sitting there. I sat

down on the floor with my back against the wall and said, "What is it, man?"

He blinked and focused on me, like it took some effort. "Oh, nothing. I just haven't had any sleep, I guess."

"In how long?"

"I don't know. A couple of days."

"A couple of days."

"Yeah."

I tried to remember what he'd looked like yesterday, succeeded, and wondered what was wrong with me that I hadn't noticed then. I said, "So, what's the problem?"

"Oh, the studio, I guess. The show. Dan. All that shit."

I said, "That's all?"

"Isn't that enough?"

I don't know why, but it hadn't really hit me before now. We had all our paintings, but so what? If we had to pack it in, we'd have blown three years for nothing. I mean *three years*. We had all started with a few bucks, anyway, and we'd poured it into keeping the studio going, and borrowed from everybody we could, and let people support us, just to see if we could make a go of it. If we threw in the towel, that would be *it*. We'd be admitting that we were just wrong — that our concept of good art with mass appeal was, as they say, bogus. Or else impractical, which in this case was the same thing.

I said, "Maybe you ought to get some sleep."

"Yeah," he said. "I probably should.'

"Or we could go get drunk."

He shook his head. I studied him. He was really miserable. It was as if it didn't matter to him that we'd been at each other's throats for the last couple of days; he was as down and out as I'd ever seen him.

I said, "Go on home, Bobby. Is your sewing machine starting these days?"

He looked up. "My what?"

I said, "Your hara kiri sumbitchi. It's running, right? Or do you still have to push it down hills?"

"Oh fuck you, Greg. At least I don't drive a bike that burns more oil than it does gas. Are they really selling oxygen tanks with those things now?"

"Yamaha," I explained to him, "should stick to making pianos."

"Can't," he said. "Kawasaki stole all the tuning forks to put on their front wheels."

I said, "At least I know when it's running. How much twine does it take to start your bike, anyway?"

" 'Bout as much as it would take to bale yours up and put it on my bitch pad."

"Look," I said. "I never said it was a *bad* sewing machine."

"Yeah, well, Kawasakis always confuse me. I can never figure out how to find the second reverse gear."

When he left, about an hour later, he was in a much better mood. I know manipulation is a dirty word, but I just couldn't manage to feel guilty.

Good deed or not, though, he'd bummed me out.

I got back to work.

4. *The Village Bride*

When I get this far into a project, it always starts to drag, no matter how excited I am. The important thing is to keep going, and, no matter how much it hurts, to take care that each stroke is applied correctly. A lot of my worst work has been done during the middle stage of a project, when I feel that, if I'm sloppy here I can make up for it later — but you can only repaint something a certain number of times before you're going to lose some of the luster, or, if you keep wiping things off with turpentine, before you hurt the canvas itself.

I took frequent breaks here; to sit back and rest, or read a bit from *A Catskill Eagle,* finally out in paperback, which I'd borrowed from David. I wondered what I could do if I were to paint a cover to a Spenser novel. Nothing very good, probably; I suspect that book covers are their own kind of thing.

I read for a bit, painted for a bit, and read some more. The important thing at this point was to keep going, and not let myself get burned out.

I was satisfied with the way the book ended. I cleaned my brushes and went home.

5. *Watson and the Shark*

Soon Csucskári came to a house and went inside. He said, "Good day, woman." (There was a woman in the house.)

She said, "Hey, Csucskári, what business have you here? You've killed the two brothers of my husband."

"What?" cries Csucskári. "Your husband must be the dragon with eight heads."

"None other," says the woman. "Now he's going to finish with you whether by fire or by water or by the point of his sword."

"Well, well," says Csucskári. "I call this a fine thank you, after I've gone to all this trouble to put the sun and the moon up in the sky. But tell me, pray, what is the sign of his coming?"

"There is no sign. There he comes."

And, indeed, the ground was trembling from the weight of the dragon. Now Csucskári was so tired from his other fights (you remember, he fought the two other dragons) that all he could think of to do was to hide. He winked at the woman in the manner of the gypsies, then hid himself under the bed.

"Heigh-ho, wife," says the dragon. "I smell a stranger

there in my house."

"There is no smell and there is no stranger you
smell. It must be your comings and goings that take you
far from your home which fill your nostrils with strange
smells." (You see, she concealed from him that Csucskári
was there.)

"Look here, woman, tell me the truth at once, or I'll
kill you outright. What is the strange smell I smell in my
house?"

"Since I cannot keep it from you, I'd better tell you.
Csucskári is in there."

"I could have guessed that it was Csucskári. And
what of your false words to me? Have you grown so fond
of him? Step forth at once, Csucskári. Tell me by what
death you choose to die."

Well, Csucskári comes out from under the bed and
dusts himself off just as if there was nothing the matter.
"You'd better ask what death you'd choose for yourself,"
he says.

"Not so fast, fellow," says the dragon. "Do you think
that because you've killed my two brothers you can do
away with me as well? Come on. Let us measure each
other's strength by the points of our swords." (You know,
he took it for granted that he would finish with
Csucskári.)

"Well, that's all right with me, but let's go outside
first, so we'll have more room."

And so they went outside to fight, though Csucskári
was so tired he could barely walk.

6. *The Morning Walk*

If there's one kind of art I hate more than any other,
it's art with a Message. This feeling grew up in me
slowly, but eventually I realized that every time I saw a
painting with some "point" to it, I didn't like it even if I

agreed with the point.

It's usually so obvious that anyone can see it right away, and so you're not going to convince anyone who doesn't already agree with you. And sometimes it's embarrassing, like somebody is making a big point about something just about everyone agrees with anyway. I mean, when I was younger the Vietnam War was an issue, and not everyone agreed. But go up to Joe Schmo on the street and say, "Hi. I'm taking a survey. Do you want nuclear war?" You know he's gonna say he doesn't, whatever his politics are. So what's the point of a work of art that says nuclear war is bad? I mean, tell me something I don't already know.

Van Gogh cared about people, and it comes through all the time in his art, but he wasn't saying, "Do this," or even, "This is the plight of such-and-such people." He was saying, "This is Truth." So how do you search for Truth? Maybe by being more interested in learning than in teaching.

Ha! And here I am, giving you a lecture on why you shouldn't lecture. Sorry, I just get upset sometimes.

I said that good art can't be propaganda, but there's another side to it. If you look at Jacques Louis David, or Diego Rivera, you'll see what I mean — these guys were going around telling you this and that and the other, but they got away with it.

Maybe it's because they were that good, and if you're good enough you can do anything. I don't know. Maybe it's that they didn't consider themselves artists, they figured they were doing propaganda, and they just did it so well they raised it to the level of fine art. So it can be done, I guess.

But I don't plan on painting a Message picture any time soon. For one thing, I'm not really sure I have anything to say.

Bones?

CHAPTER
· TEN ·

1. *THE BATHER ("AT THE DOUBTFUL BREEZE ALARMED")*

ONE OF THE arguments we had when we were trying to set up the studio was whether or not Robert got to
keep his cat, Picasso, around the place. None of us had
any inherent problems with cats, but they like to rub
against things, and Dan and David and Karen and I all
work in oils, and oil doesn't dry right away, and we wer-
en't all that pleased with adding "cat hair" to the descrip-
tion of medium on every piece. We spent an enjoyable
intoxicated evening thinking of more creative solutions to

the problem, but, when we were sober, we had to decide against poor Picasso, who now lives with Robert and harbors a grudge against the lot of us.

Most of the problems we had getting going were that kind of thing. We had the sense to get the music argued out first ("Whoever wants it quiet, wins. You can get earphones.") and some of the things we were most worried about never seemed to come up.

For instance, we all claimed to have massive egos, and so we were all nervous about the idea of accepting criticism, but once we started working, it just sort of happened.

"I don't know, Greg. I see what you're going for, but the blue is so deep that the reflections look weird."

"Yeah? Hey, Dan. Come here a minute. What do you think about the blues in here? David says they obscure the reflections."

"Mmmmm. Yeah, it wouldn't hurt if it was a bit lighter."

Or, "This makes me uncomfortable. Is that what you wanted?"

"I'm not sure. Uncomfortable how?"

"Like having my teeth drilled with a jack-hammer."

"Oh. Subtly. I see. No, I guess that wasn't exactly what I was after."

That kind of thing. One day Karen was trying to explain to me how to get a certain effect on my painting, and she finally just picked up the brush and did it. It didn't occur to me until later that I should have been upset with her. Pretty soon we were just in the habit of dabbing at each other's stuff from time to time. Not always, of course. No one has touched the Monster, I guess because I've been a little peculiar about it.

The things that give us problems are like, who forgot to turn off the coffee pot? Who spilled the paint here, and why didn't they clean it up? Who left the lights on all night? The answers, by the way, are: Robert, Dan, and, ahem, me.

All in all though, I think that the first six or eight months may have been about the most fun I've ever had. We were all so excited about each other; even Dan, The Artist Who Never Smiles, would wax enthusiastic about something one or the other of us was trying. It was great. I wish it had lasted.

2. *The Mad Woman*

The more I've worked with figures, the more I've understood why Degas liked to paint dancers. Lately, I've started to understand why he painted dancing classes. Watching a dancer, especially a ballet dancer, is like watching the human body as form, as a moving piece of sculpture. There's so much to watch. The dancers themselves are gorgeous, like perfect works of art even when standing still. The way their movements draw lines in the air can be so beautiful it almost hurts.

I should add that you can get that in acrobatics, too, or karate, which is one reason I started studying Shotokan, though only the very top masters have it so perfectly. Sensei has it—especially his side thrusts, which are so beautiful you could die—but we hardly ever get to see him really work. Jamie shows flashes when he's sparring, and Doug when he's doing Gankaku, but these are only once in a while.

When you watch ballet, take a second to follow the path of the dancer's hands, and head, or during *pas de deux;* the path of her legs as he's carrying her around the stage. I like to sit up close, and watch the movement of the muscles in the dancer's bodies, which are their own dance. Dance classes are even better than performances.

I first started to understand modern art when I was in school and I got to see lots of piss-poor artists trying to do it. The really slick stuff is pretty incomprehensible, but when you see clumsy attempts at it, you can see all the little games they're trying to play, and all the devices and tricks become obvious. Painfully obvious, in point of fact. By the same token, when you watch people trying to learn ballet, you can see what they're going through, and how they're making their bodies do those things. It's one of the best ways there is to learn about the human body.

Sex is another one, but only if you do it right.

3. *The Massacre at Chios*

I slept late Sunday and missed the weird class. Debbie took me out for breakfast at the Stewart Cafe, then came into the studio with me. We had the place to ourselves, so we necked for a while.

I lust after Debbie for her body.

Oh, that's not all, you understand, but it's a good start. She's small, with this incredible light brown hair that so far I've talked her out of cutting, and wide-set sparkling eyes that match the hair, thin eyebrows, a slightly pale complexion, high cheekbones, an impish little upturned nose, and little lines around the corners of her mouth that make her seem to be smiling all the time — which she usually is anyway.

The curve of her hip is exactly suited for the proper grip; the kind of woman you can't see without wanting to squeeze.

We continued to neck intermittently as she looked over Dan's latest, and Karen's, and Robert's. Then I went through the routine of cursing, turning off the coffee maker, scouring out the bottom of the pot, and making a fresh load. As it started dripping, I heard Debbie exclaim.

I said, "What is it?"

"This painting. My God!"

Her voice was coming from behind the screens I still had up. I walked into my area. She said, "Greg, it's wonderful."

I said, "You like it?" We call this fishing for even

more compliments.

"I love it."

"Good. So, you think it's working okay?" No, it isn't fishing for compliments, really. I don't know what it is, just that sometimes I need to hear it again and again. Debbie has always understood that without my saying anything, which is one reason I love her so much.

"It's really powerful."

"I'm glad you like it, Deb. It isn't done, and I don't know where I'm going from here. I hope I don't screw it up. The others haven't really seen it yet. It's, oh, I don't know. More ambitious than anything else I've done."

"I can see that. Wow."

In a way, I wouldn't really know anything until I got comments from the Gang, but if Debbie hadn't liked it I'd have been sunk. I mean, I trust her eye and everything, even when we don't agree on what we like, but I can't help thinking that my own work might be a blind spot for her. So, when she likes something of mine, I only half relax. The real test will be to see what the rest of the studio thinks.

Of course, the real test ought to be whether anyone buys it, but I gave up on that long ago.

She said, "Is anyone going to be showing up?"

"Hard to say. David might be in. Last Sunday everyone was, so who knows? They haven't heard the end of the story yet."

She shook her head. "You people are dedicated, I'll say that."

"Desperate," I said. "The word is desperate."

"For what?"

I sighed. "We're trying to keep the studio going, you know? We're thinking about doing a show of the bunch of us, and we don't have any money. Dan's been making noises about doing freelance work, since he's had an offer outstanding from this advertising company for months now."

She sat down on the cushions and spoke quietly. "So that *was* your resume you were typing yesterday."

I felt myself blushing. "I'm just thinking about it, that's all."

"Why? You're going to get a job so you can do a show so you can keep the studio running so you don't have to get a job?"

"Ummmm." She has this way of putting things. "It's mostly that I don't want *Dan* to have to stop working on his own stuff, you know?"

"Well, what about your work?"

"I haven't been selling anything, you know that."

"Neither has Dan."

"Yeah. Well, could we talk about something else?"

She said, "All right." She shifted in the cushions.

I said, "What am I going to do about Karen?"

Deb had a pretty good idea about the problem, because it was practically all I'd been talking about for the last few days. Deb gestured toward Karen's painting and said, "I like it."

I said, "I sort of like it, too. That isn't the point."

"Why not?"

"Because I don't *respect* it."

She was quiet for a moment, then said, "I think you're making too much of it. Your definitions of like and respect seem a little weird."

"I don't know if I'm making too big a deal out of it, or Robert is. But it's a problem, anyway. Debbie, do *you* think I'm sexist?"

She was supposed to snort and say, "Of course not." What she said, "How often do you do any of the work around the apartment?"

"That isn't sexism; that's laziness."

"Well?"

I didn't have anything to say to that. After a while, Debbie said, "You going to do some more work today?"

"When the coffee's done."

"I think it's done. Mind if I watch?"

"I love it when you watch me work. You know that."

"Yeah, but I like to ask."

I like it when she comes to the studio. I mean, most of the time she reads, so it isn't like she has her eyes fastened on me, but for some reason having her there makes me feel, I don't know, important. It might have something to do with all the money she's put in keeping me at this; but then again, maybe not.

I got my stuff ready, and by then Debbie had fixed me a cup of evil black stuff with cream and sugar, and I got down to business, feeling like Renoir creating a masterpiece.

4. *Ariadne Asleep on the Island of Nexus*

I guess it was because Debbie was there, but I felt real energetic as I faced the Monster. The energy came at the right time, too, because I needed it. I had been putting off attacking the whole area in the center behind the three figures, but now I needed to know what it would look like if I was going to get the final colors right for Artemis and Uranus.

I realized that, without thinking about it, I had decided that Apollo was going to stay nude. Well, that was all right, but I needed to put at least some clothes on Artemis, because she isn't going to run through the forest naked, is she? And Uranus was too ugly to leave naked. But the colors of their clothes had to work against the background colors, and all I had was the base.

While I thought about it, I very carefully added another coat of gloss to Apollo.

When that was done, I started mixing viridian and red, and I added some white, then a little yellow. I started trying to get a feel for the effect I wanted.

Some of the energy came back to me, then. Not an orgasmic rush like before, but I started feeling what I

wanted, and the colors built themselves and flung themselves onto the canvas, and I watched from a distance
with careful approval.

No, the fires of creation didn't explode around me,
but they burned, and that was enough.

5. *The Third of May: 1808*

Csucskári and the dragon measured their swords, and
all the clock round they fought. Each was as strong as the
other, each was as fast as the other, each was as skilled as
the other.

But Csucskári became more and more tired, until he
was almost at the end of his tether. Just as he was about
to fall, the dragon called to him, "Listen, Csucskári. It
seems to me that a valiant fighter like you is now at the
very point of death. I know that you are a great champion, so let us agree upon taking a day's rest and after it
we may start all over again in some other way."

Well, Csucskári thanked the dragon for his courtesy,
and when the day was past they went at each other again.
But even the rest of one day wasn't enough for Csucskári
to fully recover his strength, so at last he was ready to fall
again. But at just the last moment the dragon said,
"Listen, comrade, there's nothing doing. In strength
you're my equal and I am yours. So from now on we'll
turn into flames; you'll be the green flame and I shall be
the red flame."

"That's a good plan," says Csucskári, and straight-
away turned into a green flame. As he changed, he felt a
new strength come into his body, so he knew he could
keep going a while longer.

So for another day the two flames tried to smother
each other or push each other into the river (there was a
river nearby). Finally the red flame burned so strongly
that it nearly destroyed Csucskári. Just as he was about to
fail, he lifted his eyes to heaven and saw, right above him,

that there was an eagle, who was croaking away with a mournful sound.

Csucskári called to the eagle, saying, "Right you are to bemoan the ruin of the hero who is striving to fix the sun and the moon and the stars in the sky so that there may be light for all."

The eagle looked down and said, "Yes, Csucskári. When you were smaller than the hundredth part of a grain in your mother's womb, I knew that I would look down and watch you be destroyed by the dragon with eight heads."

"Never mind about that," says Csucskári, "but if you wish to live in light instead of darkness, go get as much water as you can carry in your mouth and on your wings, and let it run over the red flame."

"Well," says the eagle, "I wouldn't mind living in light instead of darkness, but I'd like to know what you'll give me if I do this for you."

And Csucskári says, "I'll give you all of the dragon's eight heads, and the flesh and hide of a whole cattle herd which he owns, and above it there will be light." But look! The red flame is still growing stronger than the green flame.

The eagle flew off, and, quick as an eagle, brought water in his mouth and on his wings and let it run over the red flame so that it began to die at once. Then Csucskári gripped his sword and at one mighty sweep cut off the eight heads of the dragon.

Then Csucskári gave the eagle the heads of the dragon and its herd of cattle, and at last lay down on the ground and rested.

6. *The Death of Marat*

Painting consists of long periods of minutes followed by short bursts of hours. In between projects, I spend a fair amount of time looking at prints, and as much time as I can manage looking at real paintings. The difference between seeing a print and seeing the painting is like the difference between seeing a postcard of Hawaii and going to Hawaii.

I do know artists who say, "I can't look at other people's work while I'm painting because their style creeps in." The first time I heard that, I did a cartoon of Gauguin's style creeping into Cezanne's work, and I called it, "Such tragedy." I thought it was pretty obvious, but the people who ought to get it never do.

I can't understand that attitude. So, someone's style has an influence on you. So what? Is his ghost going to come and push your brush around? If Cezanne's ghost wants to push *my* brush around, it's welcome to, but, really, I'm sure Cezanne's ghost has other things on its mind. Whoever you're looking at, you are the one doing the painting, and that's that.

To say, "I don't want to let anyone influence my style," is to say, "I only want to talk, I'm not interested in listening." You can say that if you want, but generally artists who say that aren't artists I'm interested in listening to.

The more I paint, the more I have to look at paintings, and the more different kinds of paintings I want to look at. Sometimes, when I'm looking at someone's work, I feel like I'm getting to know the artist, although I know that isn't the point.

I know that anyone who sees my paintings is seeing *me*, not whoever I might have been looking at the day before I painted it. And, to be honest, it's sometimes a little scary to think that anyone who wants to can just look and see you.

There is no painting so large that the artist can hide behind it.

Bones?

CHAPTER
·ELEVEN·

1. *SUNSET AFTER STORM*

ABOUT A MONTH after we started working at the studio, I got around to asking Robert why he wasn't interested in painting. He mumbled something and tried to change the subject. I brought it back. He deferred.

I said, "Oh, come on Unca Bobby. Try it one time."

"You got something against pen and ink?"

"Nope. Not a thing. You got something against paint?" He shrugged. It suddenly occurred to me that he might have some objection to painting — you know, the

way I used to object to photography, or the way Da Vinci
didn't like sculpture. On the one hand, he had the right
to object to anything he wanted to. But on the other, it
would be really weird to feel that way about *painting* for
heaven's sake. And on the third hand, how was I supposed to take comments on my work from this guy, if he
just didn't like it? I sat down and said, "Hey, what is it,
Rob? You don't like painting?"

"Sure I like it. I just don't want to do it."

"Why not?"

"What's the difference? Are we all supposed to be
doing the same things?"

"No, but if, like, it's just that you've never done any,
or —"

"No, it isn't that."

"Then what is it?"

He looked disgusted. "I'm fucking color-blind, all
right?"

I blinked, "Yeah? Really?"

"Really."

I pointed to a patch of wall and said, "What color is
that?"

He looked slightly bored. "Red."

"Yeah, you're right. How about that?"

"A lighter red."

"Well, reddish orange, but okay. How about that?"

"Ummmm . . . green?"

It was a kind of beige. After a moment he said, "Are
you through yet?"

I said, "I guess so. How come you never mentioned
this before?"

"What's the difference?"

"Well, none, I guess, but then I wouldn't have tried
to talk you into . . ." Then I said, "You know, Rob. you
can always get me or someone else to mix the colors. Or,
hell, just tell you what they look like. I mean, there are

whole libraries of books on color theory. All you have to do is keep your palette organized carefully, and maybe ask somebody once in a while and —"

"Hey, Greg?"

"Yeah?"

"How about if I just do pen and ink, all right? I *like* pen and ink. I don't feel like I'm missing anything. I am," he drew himself up and said ironically, "fulfilled as an artist. Okay?"

"Umm, yeah, sure. Okay."

And that was just about the last time we talked about it, and it really didn't make much difference, except that sometimes when we'd be arguing about so and so's work, I'd have to be careful not to say, "If you were seeing the colors I'm seeing . . ." But I couldn't get it out of my head for a long time. I mean, what did the world look like to him? What did a rainbow look like? A sunset?

Good Lord! Van Gogh! Color was at the heart of everything he did. How could Rob say he liked Van Gogh when he was seeing — who knows what? Well, maybe Van Gogh worked for him however he was seeing the colors.

Strange.

2. *Bonjour, M. Courbet*

Do you know they used to paint from plaster casts? They'd give you this plaster cast of a head, and you were supposed to use it as a model, and from this you were supposed to learn how to do faces and stuff. It isn't that you did that in addition to drawing from models; you did it instead of drawing from models.

Now, I'll tell you what would teach you to do faces: making the plaster cast. No, not a cast necessarily, but, like, clay modeling. I understand there are schools where they do that, and that makes sense. I mean, if you can *feel* the shape, you sure as hell ought to be able to draw it. And if you can draw it, you can paint it.

There's a lot of history to it, too. Do you know where they got the custom of painting halos over the heads of saints? Because the Greeks put helmets on statues of gods so birds couldn't defecate on them. I'm not kidding.

I keep meaning to try sculpture. The complexity of it has to be fun. People could look at your work from literally every possible angle. And some of the things I've seen done with it have really blown me away. I saw one veiled lady where the marble was so thin you could see the light shining through it — or maybe you just thought you could. In any case, if you looked at her *from just the right angle,* you could see her face in the light through the veil. And I saw one satyr with the most incredible musculature on his back. And the expression on his face! Can you imagine capturing the gleam in someone's eyes in *marble?*

If I were to try sculpture though, I'd have to remember that the stuff I want to do wouldn't be any more popular than the painting I'm doing, and marble, in particular, costs even more than canvas and paints, neither of which are cheap to begin with. And, being who I am, if I were to sculpt, I'd want to do it in marble.

But I can dream.

3. *The Bellelli Family*

I got to the studio late Monday afternoon, and everyone else was in. I got nods from everyone except Dan, who was really working. David and Robert, I could see right away, were getting exactly nothing done, and Karen was puttering with papers on her desk, but not painting.

I won't say there was a tension in the room; I mean, it wasn't as if something had happened, but I've seen everyone more relaxed. But, hell, what could I expect? I wasn't feeling all that hot myself. I'd spent the morning sending out resumes and calling people who always needed draftsmen.

Correction: used to need draftsmen. The first news of the day was that American Hoist had closed down its drafting operation to relocate to, I don't know, Florida or something. Not only did that remove a possible job, but they weren't taking anyone with them, so the competition would be pretty hot. I'd figured it wouldn't matter that my piece of paper was three years old, but it seemed I was wrong. I'd have to stop looking for "Draftsman" and start looking for "Entry level draftsman." In other words, when I finally break down and decide to get a job, there aren't any. Isn't life just like that?

I sat on David's table, since I knew it would be the cleanest spot in the place. The wall to his left was filled with newspaper headlines that make no sense if you don't know David. Things like, "Fireman Forced to Shave Mustache," and, "Family of Five Survive Avalanche."

I said, "So, what do we do?"

He said, "You mean about the show, and money, and that kind of thing?"

"Yeah," I said. "That kind of thing."

"I don't know."

"You could sell your Harley."

"I don't have a Harley."

"That makes it harder, then. Do you have a yacht?"

"No."

"Shit. Strike two."

We stood there for a minute, then I called out, "Hey, Unca Bobby."

He seemed to have recovered from his depression, or else my temporary cure did it. But he wasn't wearing his beret, which might or might not have meant something. When I spoke, he stood, leaned over the rail, and said "Yeah?"

"David here won't even sell his Harley for us so we

can do the show. Can you believe that?"

Robert gave me a funny look, then shrugged and went back to, I don't know, doodling I think. I knew he wasn't really working because he was sitting back. When he's working he leans forward and hunches his shoulders, and about every five minutes stretches his neck out like a giraffe with a dislocated shoulder. Every once in a while, when Debbie's in the studio, she gives him a backrub. He's said more than once that when he's rich he's going to keep her in jewels for the rest of her life.

I thought about going over to talk to Karen, but she had little "Do Not Disturb" signs in the way she was holding her arms around whatever she was doing. Just as well. I'd about decided I owed her an apology, but finding a way to phrase it that didn't make things worse wouldn't be easy.

Dan was the only one of us actually getting anything done, so I didn't want to bother him, and David didn't seem to be in a communicative mood.

My eye was drawn to the stacks of canvas leaning against the far wall. I had an itch to go over and look at them, but I decided it would just depress me.

I said, "God, we're a cheerful crew today."

The left side of David's face twitched in a feeble attempt at a smile. He said, "Guess so."

I said, "Why do you talk so much all the time?"

He said, "Verbose."

I said, "That reminds me of the Australian guy who went to visit his cousin on the outback. Well, he goes —"

"I've heard it."

"Oh." Then, "Come on, David. If you don't start amusing me pretty soon, I'm not going to have anything to do except work."

He said, "Okay, I'll abuse you a little. When are we going to get to see the Monster, anyway? I'm curious."

"Well, I don't think it's dead yet. Anyway, I hadn't

really meant to make a big thing of hiding it, it's just that I haven't gotten around to taking the screens down. I guess I'll do that tonight when I'm done working."

"Okay. I'll take a look if I'm still around, or else tomorrow. Tomorrow, probably. I think I'm going to crash early tonight."

"What? And waste all your energy?"

"That's enough, all right?"

"Sorry. Guess I'll do some work."

As I walked away I called back, "Sure you don't want to sell your Harley?"

"Maybe the yacht," he said.

I took the tubes out of the shelves and picked up my palette.

4. *Work*

I don't know why, but whenever I'm so tired I'm about to fall over, it really starts to flow. Maybe it has something to do with mental relaxation — letting my mind wander.

The way I work changes, too. When I'm tired, I work in spurts, even more than usual. Maybe a line here, then I'll sit down and read or play a game of solitaire (the latter only if Robert isn't around, because the sound of shuffling bothers him), or listen to Karen playing music, or tell one of my stories, or egg David into doing one of his cartoons.

I was feeling a little bushed anyway, and, as I sat there reading Chandler and occasionally building up a line or hiding a shadow, I was getting more tired. There were actually three things going on. One, I was tired; two, I knew that tomorrow everyone was going to be looking at what I had; and three, I was beginning to smell the end of the project. I mean, it wasn't close, but I knew I was over the hump, if you will, and getting close to putting on the final touches.

Which isn't the end either, really, because then I have to go over it again and touch up things I missed while creating it, and then I have to do that a couple more times, but the initial, creative part is the hardest, as well as the most fun, and I was just starting to feel like I'd make it.

Knowing that everyone was going to be looking at the thing and judging it always makes me nervous, but I think you can understand that. I *respect* these people. Even Karen.

I decided that the background, which was huge to begin with, was going to need more color or the figures would stand out on it and it would look too cartoony; like Gerome on a bad day.

I put the canvas on the floor and laid a thin, delicate line of almost pure white at an angle down the middle, then stepped back and studied it; shook my head. I'd wanted it to all but disappear, with the result of heightening the contrast with the colors around it, so I could go on and lighten the area around the figures, getting a better color balance, but I hadn't been quite careful enough and it was standing out too much.

I reached for the turpentine, stopped, smiled, and mixed up a dark grey that was almost what I'd used around the white, but just a little fuller and more sensuous. I played with that, and with the white, and rubbed them with my forefinger, smearing them just a bit into the canvas, and I smiled.

There was a comet in the sky.

That was enough for the day. I put the stuff away and took the screens down.

5. *For Sale (At the Bazaar)*

While Csucskári slept, the wife of the dragon with twelve heads went to see the wife of the dragon with ten heads. They talked in the way of wives for a while, then they said, "What should we do about this Csucskári, who has killed our husbands?" They thought about tying him up and throwing him in the river, but they were afraid he would burst his bonds and escape. They thought about throwing him into fire, but they were afraid he would put the fire out with water he had saved in his mouth from being thrown into the river.

At last they decided to see the wife of the dragon with eight heads, so they set off to her house. When they got there, they talked for a while in the way of wives, then said, "What should we do about this Csucskári, who has killed our husbands?" The wife of the dragon with eight heads said, "We should go at once to see our old father-in-law, who will know how to deal with this rascal."

So they marched off to do that. Meanwhile, Csucskári wakes up, and goes walking down the road. When the wives got to their old father-in-law, they paid their respects and passed the time with him as good daughters will, then they said, "What should we do about this Csucskári, who has killed our husbands?"

The old dragon asked his eldest daughter-in-law, "Well, my dear daughter, what curse would you put upon Csucskári who has killed your husband, the dragon with twelve heads?"

"Well, dear father," she says, "only this: I would bring hunger upon him and then make him eat a loaf of bread of which a single bite would make him burst into twelve pieces."

"Right you are, my eldest daughter-in-law. Well, what about you, my second daughter-in-law? What curse would you put upon Csucskári who killed your husband, the dragon with ten heads?"

"Only this: Within a mile from the place hunger comes upon him, I would make him thirst so much he would almost perish from it. Then I would make him pass a well so that when he drinks of it, its water would make him burst into ten pieces."

"Right you are, my second daughter-in-law. So what about you, my youngest daughter-in-law? What pains would you put upon Csucskári who killed your husband, the dragon with eight heads?"

"I would make him pass a pear tree laden with the biggest and finest pears so that when he'd take a bite into a pear it would make him burst into eight pieces."

Oh, there is something I forgot to mention. When Csucskári woke up and started walking down the road, he saw the three wives of the three dragons, and so he followed them. So now while this was going on, he slipped into the house and found the old tom-cat and shook its insides out and slipped into its skin. Then he jumped into the lap of the youngest daughter-in-law.

The youngest daughter-in-law said to the wife of the old dragon, "Well, dear mother, what curse would you put upon Csucskári who killed your three sons?"

"As for me," said the hag, "I'm going to sit on the shovel blade and ride after him and burn his buttocks."

Hearing this, Csucskári defecated on the lap of the youngest daughter-in-law and took off.

The old dragon said, "We may as well go to hell now. All of us. Csucskári has overheard us talking. There is nothing we could do against him."

6. *The Angelus*

I have, on occasion, asked myself, "What's the point?"

I don't know if I have a good answer for that one. I mean, sometimes it's obvious and straightforward, like that propaganda I was talking about earlier. If Goya makes you feel pity for the victims of oppression, it may change your attitudes and so on. But my problem is that I can't make myself — or I just don't want to make myself — think in terms of large numbers of people. I think in terms of individuals. I'm not saying this is good, but there it is. When I'm feeling snide, I say that the only masses I think about are the ones on the canvas.

But sometimes when I'm not feeling snide I'm taken with a sense of futility that has nothing to do with the fact that I couldn't sell a painting for a nickel to a grade school. It's a more general futility, that has to do with, "What's the *point* of this art I'm so proud of, or at least, that I'm so involved in?" I mean, Raphael's work has survived invasion, uprising, and war, and it still affects me. Rembrandt's works are of such a different age from ours that there is almost no similarity, but they can still move me to tears. When I look at my own work, I get the feeling that any little breeze that blows through the world will remove any meaning they might have.

This may be the most depressing of my many depressing thoughts.

Something like nuclear war hardly qualifies as a "little breeze," and it is incredibly asinine to worry that, if the whole world were destroyed, my art wouldn't be "relevant." But I'm asinine. And there are certainly things short of nuclear war that would change the way people look at art, because art always reflects the society that gave it birth; the great artists are the ones who create works that transcend that society, and I know I'm not doing that.

Of course, the answer is that if the world changes, and society changes, I'll change too, and I won't be doing the same things any more. But I look at "Mirror, Mirror," or some of my other works that I'm proud of, and I contemplate a world of food riots, or nuclear war, or something, and I say, "What could I possibly offer such a world?"

Once again, I guess, I'm just worrying too much. Don't listen to me, it's just the outcry of a man worried about something far more important than the fate of

Spanish insurgents, or the threat of nuclear catastrophe, or the dangers of World War III. To wit: will Dan like my painting?

Sheesh. Here I am talking about evoking pity, and I spend my time asking for it. That's not how it ought to be. I'm sorry. Ignore me. The pity I want to invoke isn't for me personally, any more than my goal is to make you feel pity for the underprivileged of the world. The latter is a worthy thing, and I hope you feel it, but my brush is too small to paint it.

I want you to feel pity for Uranus, who dies that a gate may be opened, but dies nevertheless. And for Artemis, who, I now see, has cared for him. And for Apollo, who must demean himself by taking a life. I want you to feel pity; maybe even make you cry. Crying is not a sadness, because as the tears leave our eyes, some of the pain leaves, too, and we can go on living, and so feel more pain, yes, but some joy, as well.

The line between sanity and madness may be only the ability to shed a few tears.

Bones?

CHAPTER
·TWELVE·

1. SYMPHONY IN WHITE, NO. 1

YOU'VE PROBABLY noticed by now that I'm a bit in awe of Dan. Dan noticed it too, about a year and a half ago, I think. He took me out for a drink at a strip joint on Lincoln (there were no dancers at the time) and tried to explain that I was making him nervous. I could see he was really working hard not to offend me.

I said, "All right, Dan. I'll lighten up."

He said, "You know what I'm talking about?"

"I guess so."

"It's like you're putting me on a pedestal."

"Well, I think you're that good."

He looked extremely uncomfortable. "It's not like I'm not pleased that you think I'm good. I'm flattered. But for one thing, if you think everything I do is wonderful, you aren't going to be able to point out my problems."

"That's true, I'm not," I said cheerfully.

Dan looked frustrated and unhappy. No, I wasn't trying to make things as hard for him as possible, but he was making *me* unhappy, and I didn't know how to handle him any better than he knew how to handle me.

He said, "But Greg, I respect you. I want your opinions, and you can't give them to me if you think everything I do is perfect."

I stopped and thought for what felt like a long time. Then I said, "Let me try to explain this. This isn't easy."

"Go ahead."

"All right. It's like this. Sometimes an artist will just win me over. Like Delacroix, or Rembrandt, or Van Gogh."

"Nothing wrong with your taste," he muttered.

I continued, "I know, intellectually, that Van Gogh wasn't perfect; nobody is perfect. But it's just something that happens to me that I flip out for someone. When that happens, I can't be objective anymore. When I see something that any reasonable person would call clumsy, or bad use of form, or improper balance, I find myself saying, 'That jars. I wonder why he did that? What was he going for?'

"I know that isn't the best way to look at a painting to get the most out of it, but it isn't something I can control. Well, I'm sorry, but that happened with you. It wasn't any one piece that did it, either, but seeing all those studies of the riverfront, and the 'Showboat,' and just one thing after another.

"I'm sorry it makes you uncomfortable, but that's just how it is."

He shook his head, like he hadn't even been listening. "Don't you see that that blinds you to the works you like?"

"Yeah. But I'll bet I enjoy them more than you, when you spend all your time picking them apart to see how they got this or that effect. I just enjoy them."

"I don't think so. I think you can get more out of a painting the more you understand it."

"But do you ever, like, *fall into* a painting? Get lost in it?"

"Sure. That's how I feel what's right and what's wrong with it. It isn't as if I turn my brain off just because I'm looking at a painting."

I started to argue, then changed my mind. "Yeah, maybe you're right. We could argue about it all week. It doesn't matter."

Since then I've tried not to slobber over his work quite so much. It smears the paint.

But, damn, he's good.

2. *Beata Beatrix*

I used to play electric bass, and some friends and I had a rock band while I was in college. It played regularly, like every three months or so. We were never very good, but we had fun playing frat parties and stuff. I used to sing a couple of songs a night. No one ever accused me of being a good singer, but I really enjoyed it.

I had a lot of trouble playing bass and singing at the same time. There's just too much disconnection between what your hands are doing and what your throat and mouth are doing for me to ever get good at it. There were a few songs, though, that were simple enough so I could just put my hands on automatic and think about singing.

When you're singing, you can be thinking about one of two things (aside from your chances of making the brunette in the white tee-shirt): you can be thinking of how you use your voice, or you can be thinking about what the song means. The problem is, you really ought to do both, and I was nowhere near a good enough singer for that, which is why I only sang a couple of songs a night.

I mentioned earlier that I have to keep thinking about technique; the bare mechanics of painting. Well, mostly that's what happens, but other times I forget about it and just get lost in the work. The problem is, I should really be doing both.

Every once in a great while I hit a place. I call it a "place" because that's how I think of it; like I've managed to climb into this room where the mechanics are laid out like little knobs, or like a puppeteer's strings, and I sit there in back and pull them or turn them just as calmly as you please. Meanwhile, outside the room, all the thoughts and feelings and hopes and emotions that make up my ideal of that painting are pouring out into it, and I understand fully and perfectly what I'm after and how I'm going to get it.

I can never quite understand it after I leave the room, and speculating on what goes on in there is as fascinating as it is useless. But I know it happens.

I wonder if Billie Holiday ever felt that, or some form of it? Does Dave Van Ronk ever feel it? Did Bessie Smith? Does Spider John Koerner? I'll probably never know.

But when it happens to me, brush in hand, I'm singing.

3. *Prisoners From the Front*

I was in early Tuesday, before everyone except Dan. Robert and Karen came in half an hour later. I was just sort of wandering around and trying not to look like I was biting my nails. After what seemed to be forever, Dan stretched out his arms, put his brushes down, and wandered over — to Robert's area. He looked down at a drawing of Malcolm X that Robert had been doing off and on for the last week, and, I guess, had finally completed. I went over there too. Hell, I could wait. I wasn't quite dying yet.

Robert was saying, "He's just always fascinated me, you know? As a character. My widow first got me interested in him from a book she read." Robert always refers to his ex-wife as "my widow." I finally asked him about it one day and he said, "Well, I might as well be dead as far as she's concerned."

Dan was saying, "Yeah, you really got involved, didn't you?"

"At the end," he said. "Finally. That's how I managed to finish it."

I looked at it, and saw right away what Dan meant, although I wouldn't have put it quite that way. But there was a certain *aliveness* to it that hit you. I thought he could have done a smoother job on the cheekbones, which looked a bit forced and unnatural. I also didn't agree with his decision to show fully half of the torso. But those were both minor points.

I said, "I really like it."

"Good," said Robert, meaning it.

Dan said, "Can you make the forehead just a little more detailed? I don't like losing that." I smiled to myself. I hadn't caught that, but Dan rarely misses anything.

"Sure," said Robert. "Anything else?"

"I like the eyes a *lot*," I said. "I think that's what makes it work." Dan and Karen muttered what sounded like agreement. "I do think you could get away with showing less of his torso. I think it detracts from his strength."

He thought about that, then nodded. "Yeah, you're right."

I was about to mention the other problem when

Karen turned to me and said, "What do you think of the cheekbones?"

I said, "Yeah, I'd like to see the line thinner, I think, so there's more definition. This fades into the crinkles around his eyes, and . . . didn't he wear glasses, by the way?"

"Yeah, but I figured I could get him better without them."

"That might have been a mistake," said Dan, "if you were working from a picture where he wore them. That may be why the cheekbones are weak."

Robert seemed unhappy. "You think I ought to draw the glasses in?"

Dan said, "Or fix the cheekbones some other way. Whatever you want."

Robert said, "I don't want to change that. It takes all the character out of his face.

I groaned to myself, and caught a glimpse of Karen doing the same thing. Dan said, "You've got his character in his eyes and his mouth. The cheekbones just look weird."

That was an overstatement, but I figured excusable this time. Robert said, "That line, down to his chin, is what gives me the feeling of determination."

I said, "No, that's a parody of determination. It's almost a caricature. Well, not that bad, but I don't think it works."

Robert said, "You want me to remove everything that makes the drawing unique and interesting."

Karen gave an exasperated sigh and said, "You're right, Robert. We admit it. We're all jealous of you, and our only goal for the last three years has been to keep you from producing your best work, so you don't put us all to shame."

He flushed. "All right, goddamnit, I'll change the fucking cheekbones."

I could feel Dan clenching his fists, although in fact I don't think he moved. I said, "Look, Robert, that isn't the point. You can do whatever you want. It's *your* drawing. The point is that it's our opinion, or at least mine, that thinning out that line will improve it. So we're stating our opinion. You don't *have* to listen, and you don't have to change it if you don't agree. But you said a long time ago that you wanted our comments on your work, and there it is. Don't be so fucking absolute about everything."

Robert mumbled something and said, "All right," and withdrew into himself. Closed up tight, snap, like a hymnal at the end of services. David came in right then, thank God, which gave me an excuse to leave while Karen and Dan muttered a few more compliments about the drawing — which it deserved, although I'm sure Robert couldn't believe that any more.

I walked over to David and said quietly, "If you're going to bitch about the cheekbones in Robert's drawing, at least wait a few days."

"Why?"

"I'll explain later."

"Okay. I see the screens are down."

"Yeah."

"Mind if I have a look at it?"

When I turned, I saw that Dan and Karen had left Robert's area and were both studying the Monster. I felt my stomach drop. The blow-up with Robert had at least distracted me. David walked over and joined them. I was going to have three of them at once look at it. Oh, lucky me.

Karen spoke first. "I think I like it," she said.

I said, "You think?" still feeling queasy.

"Well, it's one of those paintings where I'm not going to know until you're done, but I like your subject, and you're doing some interesting things with it. There's some power there, but I don't know if it'll diffuse when you've completed it. You sure have gotten a lot done since last week, though. Sheesh.''

I started to feel a little better, realizing that this was what had been worrying me; I knew it had been going quickly, but I also knew that could be either a good or bad sign. Dan was nodding to what Karen said. Okay. They didn't know any more than I did. Well, it could be worse.

Then David said, "Ummm, Greg, is that deliberate?" And my stomach dropped three stories.

"Is what deliberate?"

He pointed to the wolf. "That's exactly the same wolf, in the same posture, that you used in the Jack London thing."

I stared at it. I stared some more. I felt myself flushing. I covered my face. "Jesus Christ," I said. "Can I go home now?"

Dan said, "Big deal. So you fix it. So what? In any case, there's no law that says you can't have the same thing —"

"But that's *blatant*. My God, how did I miss that? It was the subject of the whole painting." When no one answered, I said, "Drugs. It must be drugs. Either using them or not using them, I don't know. Jesus. Would you guys mind not looking at it any more? No, never mind. I'm going to go kill myself now. Wait, I can't until I've fixed that. Holy Jesus Christ with Twelve Saints Running."

David laughed, then said, "By the way, I *really* like the approach you're taking, with the varying brush strokes. I think that's working."

"I agree," said Karen.

"I mostly agree," said Dan.

"Mostly?"

"Greg, have you ever studied pointillism?"

I looked at the upper left, just to the right of the

gate, and said, "Well, no."

"You should practice it before you use it. That just looks like a mess."

I felt myself flushing. "I'm not trying to do Signac. I want it to be kind of vague."

Dan said, "It doesn't look vague; it looks like you don't know what you're doing."

I said, "You guys agree?"

Karen said, "Well, I don't think it's all that bad, but yeah, it could use some work."

David said, "I guess it could. It's just that that's one of Dan's specialties, so he's sensitive to it."

Dan seemed to be getting seriously annoyed. "I know something about it, so I can see when it's done wrong. Most people might not know what you were trying to do, but it won't convey what you want it to."

None of the others said anything, so I could have ignored him or argued more, but I heard echoes of the scene with Robert in what I was about to say, so I refrained.

What would I do without you, Unca Bobby?

4. *In the Sun*

I mixed blue with black, then added some more blue but didn't mix it, just letting it swirl there. Karen had turned me on to that, I think from one of her classes. It's a nice effect, because you're going to end up with an area that's blue, with pieces of a deeper blue, but you can't control exactly where the swirls end up. The result is an almost haphazard appearance, and it can do really nice things for the tone.

I played around with that some, still trying to strengthen the background. Then I stopped, smiled, and went back to my palette. I built up a pastel grey, really pale, took hold of my quarter inch brush, gave a short prayer to the Muses, and attacked the whole center section of the background. During the course of it I destroyed the wolf, which made me feel better at once.

I continued, wiping out little details that, to be honest, I hadn't put all *that* much time into creating. They went away even more easily than they'd come, and when I was finished, there was, functionally, no background at all.

Of course, that's impossible, there's *always* some background, even if it's unpainted canvas, but, except for the suggestion of mountains in one corner and the gate in the other, the basic backing of the canvas was almost a complete wash. I touched it up here and there with my black-blue swirls —frankly, because I didn't want to waste them after having built them. And they looked nice.

Then I darkened the grey and added some viridian (viridian? trust me — it worked) and painted in a different wolf with a different orientation. It wasn't quite as nice a wolf this time, but it was staring at Uranus and baring its teeth, which I decided helped direct the painting.

Okay, even trade, and I wouldn't have to feel stupid dealing with people who knew the other work. There was a moment, then, when it occurred to me to wonder why I wanted the wolf there at all. I mean, why a wolf? Why not a duck? I didn't have any special significance in mind for it; not consciously, at any rate.

While I was trying to decide about that, I realized that I still hadn't resolved what was most worrying me about the painting. To wit, the over-all effect. I mean, a painting should have as many nice touches as possible, but it needs an over-all theme, or point, or direction. Usually that's the most obvious thing, but because of the way I was doing this one, I was still waiting for it to emerge.

I stared at the canvas some more, but nothing magically appeared for me. Maybe tomorrow.

It was pretty late by then, but I took some time to set up a junk canvas and practiced pointillism before I went home.

5. *La Charmeuse*

Csucskári walked back until he came to the house of the dragon with eight heads. He went inside and found a bushel of pears. Then he walked until he came to the house of the dragon with ten heads. He went inside and found a bottle of wine. Then he walked until he came to the house of the dragon with twelve heads. He went inside and found a loaf of bread.

He carried these until he came to the cave where the sow lay with her nine piglets. He walked through the cave until he was near the sleeping troll and the boar. Then he walked through the forest until he came to his brothers, who were waiting for him next to a brook.

"Well, how are you, brothers?" he asked.

"Since you are asking us, brother," they said, "we are hungry."

"You say you are hungry," said Csucskári, and he brings out the loaf of bread, the bushel of pears, and the bottle of wine. The two brothers eat their fill, but Csucskári being a *taltos* doesn't touch anything, neither food nor drink.

When they had finished eating, Csucskári took out his sword. "See here, brothers. This sword has slain the dragon with twelve heads, the dragon with ten heads, and the dragon with eight heads. Now you must swear upon its hilt that you will let me be first in everything we do from now on, or otherwise you will perish by a horrible death. But I have the sun, the moon, and the stars in this little box in my pocket. Hereafter I shall win myself a royal palace, and until then our lives are still at stake."

So Bagoly and Holló swear an oath on the hilt of the

sword that they will allow Csucskári to be first in all they do, and after that they set out upon the road.

6. Rainy Season in the Tropics

I asked one of my professors once why he always talked about painters "executing" a painting. That seemed like such a stupid way to put it. You paint a picture. Or maybe you "do" a painting. "Execute" is so pretentious, you know?

He didn't have any good answers for me, but then, he didn't have any good answers to much of anything. He had strong ideas on what was good and bad, and I don't think we agreed on anything more recent than 1930. The other thing I remember about him is that he made absolutely no distinction between, "This is good," and "I like this." The only conclusion I could come to was that he liked everything that was good and disliked everything that was bad. Even if you attach a posthumous "In my opinion" to that kind of attitude, it still stinks.

A work of art isn't automatically good because an art historian likes it, or bad because he doesn't. I have opinions on what is good and what is bad and why, even if they aren't as expert as they ought to be. Furthermore, I know what moves me — what hits me where I live.

There are some paintings I've seen where I've said, "Well, it isn't very good, but I like it." I don't think I'd better give any examples in case the perpetrators come across this, but I've seen them. There are lots and lots of paintings that make me go, "Well, it's very good, but I don't like it." Hell, Munch's "The Scream" is a masterpiece any way you cut it, and I'd die to be able to paint like that. It is very, very good. I don't happen to like it.

So shoot me.

Bones?

CHAPTER
•THIRTEEN•

1. *THE ARTIST'S STUDIO*

YOU MAY BE GETTING the impression that Dan and I are like the gonzo killers — paint paint paint, while the others are lazy slugs. No, it isn't really like that. We learned about each other's styles pretty quickly.

Dan works constantly, though slowly. He comes in early, usually mid-morning, five or six days a week, paints slowly and carefully for a few hours, eats, paints some more, and goes home. If he finishes a three-month project at four in the afternoon, he'll pick up another canvas and start the next one. He always knows exactly how long the projects will take, too, so he'll always have a canvas ready in time. Sometimes that impresses me as much as his work.

Robert comes in at all sorts of odd hours, and sits around the studio doing nothing, or runs out for a walk around the neighborhood, and then all of a sudden he'll pick up his illustration board and fire off the stuff so fast I can hardly watch his hand move. Then he'll stare at it for a while and erase a few lines, gradually sinking back into quiescence.

Karen is a bit like Dan. She shows up in the early afternoon Monday through Friday, only rarely on weekends. She works slowly and steadily for a few hours, takes a break, then works some more, takes another break, and like that until she goes home. The reason she gets so much more done than Dan is that she chooses subjects that don't require intensive concentration. She'll usually finish a 36 x 24 canvas in a week or a week and a half.

David works whenever he feels like it. You can never guess when he is or is not going to be in. When David is drawing he sits at his table and reads, or stares off into space for hours at a time, then does a few lines, then stops. When he's painting instead of reading or sitting there, he takes strolls around the studio, apparently in a grey fog, looking as if he's going to bump into something. When a painting is going badly he likes to get us into arguments so we make him mad, then he storms off and slashes dark colors onto the canvas in broad, thick strokes. I don't think he knows he's doing that, but the results are usually pretty good. What really kills me is that both he and Karen sometimes have three or four projects going at the same time. I could never work that way.

I like to work late. If I had my way, I'd show up about nine or ten in the evening, work all night, and go home about nine or ten in the morning. But Debbie works from mid-afternoon until eight, so I try to make my schedule match hers, just so I get to see her every once in a while. Other than that, I'm sort of like David at the beginning of a project, like Dan or Karen in the middle, and like Robert at the end. I have to tell you this because "Death of Uranus" has been funny for me in how fast it's gone. I hope it turns out all right.

2. *Gloucester Farm*

A couple of my friends take cooking very seriously. I respect them for it, because I know they've worked hard at it, and because I've had their food. Oh, don't worry; I'm not about to start in about whether cooking is a real art or only a craft. At least, not *exactly*.

What's interesting about contrasting these two guys is their attitudes. One of them turns up his nose at people who just throw things that look good into a pot, cook it, and eat it. This annoys me every once in a while, because that's what I do.

The other guy doesn't have this attitude. As far as he's concerned, food is for eating, and if he happens to enjoy spending eight hours in the kitchen to prepare this incredible dish, well, that's just how he likes to do things and so what?

I'll eat anything either one of them cooks, though. I have to wonder just how much difference attitude makes. Probably not a whole lot.

3. *The Coming Storm*

· I felt good after training Wednesday. We worked on Kanku-dai, which is one of my favorite katas (kata? What's the plural of kata?), and Sensei had really torn into me about what all I was doing wrong — which turned out to be just about everything — I was muscling it here, I had no connection to the ground there, I didn't understand explosion or focus or breathing. This meant I was making enough progress that it was worth his time to criticize me, so I was pleased.

They were all there and talking when I came in — Robert, Karen, David, Dan. All sitting around and gabbing right by the door. Karen had taken my spot at David's table. I said, "Okay, goddamit, man is a territorial animal and you is in my territory."

She got off the table without making any remarks, which either meant she was pissed at me or that she was distracted. I studied her face and decided on distracted. As I sat down, David said, "We're trying to figure out the show."

I squelched an urge to say that my uncle still had a barn. I said, "Are there any ideas at all for raising the money?"

David shook his head.

I said, "So, what's there to talk about?"

David said, "Dan has suggested that we kill the whole thing."

I swallowed, not wanting to understand. "The show idea?"

"The studio."

"I didn't propose it," said Dan. "I just suggested we think about it. It isn't as if we've failed — we've done a lot of good stuff. The question is, are we going anywhere? Maybe we're already dead, and it's just a matter of making it official."

"Maybe not," I said.

"I agree," he said. "Maybe not. I'm just saying we ought to think about it."

"I'd rather not."

"Why?"

"Because I like working with you guys. I think I'm dong good stuff — or as good as I'm capable of. I don't see how breaking up the studio is going to make me do anything any better."

"How will you know unless you try?"

That stopped me for a second, then I said, "What's the point? All I want is a place to paint with people whose opinions I trust. I think that way I'll be able to do my best work."

Dan shrugged. "I'm not saying that we ought to do it. But I've been thinking, since we're having all these money problems, that maybe we ought to just think things over."

"You think things over," I said. "I'll paint." No one except Dan had said anything, but I had the feeling that they all pretty much agreed with me. After a bit, I said, "All right, what do you mean by 'going somewhere,' anyway?"

"Well, what's our goal?"

I blinked. "Our goal? I don't remember setting anything like a goal. We just figured we'd all be able to do our best work if we worked together."

"Okay. Do you think that's still true?"

"Yes."

He shook his head. "Have you *thought* about it?"

I shrugged. "Not a whole lot."

"Well, like I said, maybe we should think about it."

There wasn't anything to add to that, so I stood up and walked back to my area and spread my equipment out, then decided that I was too worked up to paint, so I got a cup of coffee to calm me down.

That was a joke.

But I did get a cup of coffee, and when I came back into the room, David was staring at his mother, Robert was looking at Karen's "Wheelock Park," which was coming along pretty quickly, and Dan was back at his canvas. I walked outside to get some air, did so, came back in.

I decided I was feeling better, and was probably ready

to work. I wandered over to ask Karen and Robert what they thought of Dan's suggestion. Before I opened my mouth, Karen turned to me and gave me a smile. "What do you think?" she asked, indicating her canvas.

I glanced at it and started to answer. I stopped. I could feel Robert's eyes on me. I swallowed. I looked at the painting again. It was a spring study, with a big naturalistic tree in the foreground that was just budding, and shadows sprouting from it onto green, green grass, and the clouds in the awfully blue sky were light and puffy. Off to the side was the base of the naval cannon, which was pointed off into nowhere and looking very non-threatening; more like a totem than a weapon. The words, "It's pretty," sprang to my lips, but Robert was still watching me so I didn't say them.

I said, "It lacks balls."

Karen blinked. "What do you mean?"

"I mean, so what? So there's a park on a nice day. What's the point?"

"Why does there have to be a point? I wanted to do a painting of a park."

I shrugged to give myself time to think. I was already regretting having opened my mouth, but I'd done it and I couldn't quit now. I thought over what she said and looked at the painting some more. I told her, "If you're going to do a pretty landscape, at least leave the viewer something to do. In this you aren't suggesting anything, you're just making the statement, 'It was a nice day at the park.' Well, so what?"

She said, "So I painted it, that's what. There isn't anything to suggest because I'm not getting at anything. You want to throw in a dead cat, or what? I was at the park, and it was a nice day, and I saw that tree with the cannon, thought it would make a nice painting, did the sketches. Don't you think it makes a nice painting?"

I said, "Yeah. It's nice." I put a little emphasis on the

word, "nice."

I put a little too much emphasis on the word, "nice."

Karen said, "Well fuck you too, then," grabbed her green woolen purse and stormed out of the studio.

I could feel Dan and David looking at me. Robert was looking at the door out of which Karen had run. I opened my mouth to say, "Okay, is that what you wanted?" But for once I managed not to say it.

After a while, David said, "Well, I guess that's up front."

I winced.

Dan said, "Not to rub it in, Greg, but do you see my point?"

I said, "Huh?"

"Would this have happened two years ago? If we were really doing something worthwhile, would this have even come up?"

I said, "Shit. I don't see why not. All that happened —"

David said, "Look, let's not talk about it right now, okay?" He was looking at Robert who was still kind of staring at the door.

"Yeah," said Dan.

I walked back to my area and picked up my paints. If I could have had one wish, it would have been that I'd left my screens up.

4. *Eva Gonzales*

I picked up a quarter-inch brush and put it down. I picked up an eighth-inch brush, then traded it for the palette knife and toyed with the ivory black for a while, then put my paints down.

All the books say that being miserable is supposed to inspire you to create great art. Shit. Being miserable makes me want to go to sleep, not paint. I don't think

Rubens was miserable a day in his life. If he could paint
masterpieces while he was happy, I guess I can be excused
for not being able to paint while I'm miserable.

I puttered around for a while, darkening the outline
of the wolf, then I cleaned my tools, put things away, and
went home.

5. *Flight and Pursuit*

All that day Csucskári led his brothers on and on, not
stopping for anything. Nor would he answer when they
asked where Csucskári was leading them. At last when
they stopped and rested Bagoly said, "Come now, brother,
can't you tell us where we're going, and why we haven't
yet put the sun, the moon, and the stars up into the
heavens?"

"We are waiting for the wives of the three dragons,
who will try to kill us. Until they do, and I have defeated
them, it isn't safe for us to stop for more than a few minutes. If they find us resting, we've had it."

So after a moment they stood up again, and walked
on and on until the eldest brother, Holló, says, "Oh,
brother, the most horrible hunger has come upon me, and
I think I will die upon this spot if I do not eat."

So Csucskári says, "Do not worry, brother. I see a
loaf of bread yonder there. It won't take us long to get
there and then we can have our fill of it. Just keep your
courage up till we come to that bread. But remember, you
must let me go first."

Well, pretty soon they reach the loaf. Csucskári takes
it in one hand, and instead of breaking it to feed them, he
pierces it with his spear (you remember; he had the spear
for fighting the boar). Well, as soon as he pierced it the
spear broke into twelve pieces, but red blood came forth
from the bread, and that was the end of the wife of the
dragon with twelve heads.

They had been traveling some little time after that when Bagoly said, "Csucskári, I hate to burden you with my troubles after all you've been through, but the most terrible thirst has come upon me, that I fear I shall die from it."

"Do not worry, brother. I see a well over there. We are going to have a drink from it, but I must go first."

When they reached the well, Csucskári pulled out his sword and struck the well with it. Well, the sword breaks into ten pieces, but a great crack appears in the wall of the well, and red blood flows forth from it. And that was the end of the wife of the dragon with ten heads.

They walked on until they came to a pear tree. Then Holló says, "Look, Csucskári. I see a pear tree yonder there. How I wish I could pick a pear or two for myself."

"Do not worry, my dear brother. In less than a minute you can pick a pear or two for yourself, but I must go there first."

Then he goes up to the tree and takes a pear down, and with his pocket knife he cuts the pear in two. And, lo! red blood flows forth from the pear, the knife breaks into eight pieces, and the tree cracks and falls. And that was the end of the wife of the dragon with eight heads.

They walked on a little more, until suddenly Csucskári looks behind him and sees the hag riding up on a shovel hot enough to burn her buttocks.

Bagoly turns to Csucskári and says, "Come, Csucskári, what now? How will you defeat her?"

And Csucskári shakes his head and says, "She is too much for me. I can't."

6. *Impression: Sunrise*

I keep talking about how bad my profs were. You really shouldn't pay that much attention. I learned a lot from them. It's just that what really sticks in my mind are all the things I didn't like, or didn't agree with, or didn't understand. I mean, those guys were better than I'll ever be at understanding why a painting has the effect it has, and what makes it good or bad; I'd be a lot better off if I understood more. But as soon as they try to generalize, an alarm goes off in my head.

One guy (for the record, none of the rest of the profs agreed with him) divided artists into those who looked in and those who looked out — that is, those who wanted to understand nature, and those who wanted to understand themselves. He said every other division was secondary to that.

If you try to show the world, it's still *you* trying to show the world, and if you're looking inside yourself, you're still part of the world, aren't you?

I can, if I want to, try to show the world as if I weren't a part of it. That's *easy* with paint. When you stand there contemplating what you want to paint, a kind of frame forms itself between your eyes and the subject so you can get an idea of what will appear on the canvas. This frame not only blocks out everything else, but separates you from the subject itself. When you do that it becomes easy to pretend that nature is "out there" and you are "in here."

What's harder is to say, "No, I'm a part of this. I'm showing nature, and nature includes me." I don't mean to paint yourself into the work — although God knows it's been done and mostly badly — but to work at *expressing* it. To try to understand, "What is this *thing* I'm painting? How can I understand it with my brush and my colors?" The process of trying to capture it — now there's a *good* way of putting it —involves you in it.

This is especially true when painting people, by the way. I should do more portraits. Thing is, I'm hung up on movement. Maybe I have the soul of an illustrator, not an artist. No, on second thought, if I wanted to be an illustrator, I'd always be seeing things I want to illustrate, instead of —

Of —

What is it I *do* see?

I'm not really sure, now that I think of it. I guess what I respond to are *moments*. I'll see something that will evoke a reaction like, "Yeah, that's it. That catches it. I have to bring that out so people can see it." Maybe I *should* try photography.

I don't want to deal with appearances. The point about the appearance is that it can show you what's underneath, and that's what I'm after. I have no reason to think I'm going to succeed, or even to think that I'll be able to produce good paintings while I try.

But that's my goal. I just want you to understand.

Bones?

CHAPTER
•FOURTEEN•

1. *MENDING THE NET*

I REMEMBER when, in karate, I learned how to do front kicks. I'd been doing them, sort of, for more than a year, and I didn't realize I was doing anything wrong. For the whole year, Sensei had been saying (among other things), kick with the knee, just let the lower leg relax, and manipulate the ankle so you attack with the ball of your foot. And, more and more, kick with the knee, kick with the knee.

One day, between kicks number four and five out of a

set of ten at medium speed, I kicked with the knee. That is, I let my lower leg relax and concentrated on getting the knee out there, and *bam*. The kick *flew*. It was fast, and strong, and felt so good I almost couldn't stand it. I was astounded at what I'd done, but after that, well, I had it, and that was that.

What's funny is that I hadn't done anything other than what Sensei had been telling us to do for more than a year, yet when it came, it was like a Zen moment of enlightenment. I wanted to share it with some friends at the doj, but I couldn't. Why? Because all I could say was, "You kick with your knee; just let your lower leg relax."

Everything I discovered like that; I try to listen to my teachers, and follow their directions, and sometimes I even think I have it, and then one day, *bam*.

In one life-drawing class, using pencil and paper, the prof gave us a long lecture on light. A lot of what he told us were raw facts — like the math or physics you use to determine the length of a shadow, and how to represent the shadings of light with only a pencil. But there were other things he was saying, especially about the old Dutch painters, that I only thought I understood. You must always have a light source in mind, and that affects everything on the canvas, even if the light is diffuse and the source isn't explicit. Okay, that was simple enough, right? Wrong.

I only understood it one day about eighteen months ago, working on a study of the alley in back of the studio. Just, all of a sudden, for no reason, I understood. The effect of the sun from my right permeated the whole canvas, brightening some spots just a little, darkening others by only the tiniest amount, but it was there, I understood it. I almost had an orgasm.

I wanted to talk to David about it, but all I could think of to say was, "You always have a light source in mind, and that affects everything on the canvas." So I didn't say anything, but, hell, my paintings have been better since then.

My front kicks are pretty good, too.

2. *King Cophuetа and the Beggar Maid*

I took some theater courses while I was at the "U". I needed a certain number of credits, and not all of them had to be the dull stuff, and I figured theater would be pretty easy. I was right, for a change; it was pretty easy. If I'd been serious about it, it would probably have been more difficult, but I was just putting in time.

Yet, I learned a few things that stayed with me. Some of it was little stuff that's been helpful; I'm the one who sets up all the lights in the studio, because I understand lighting. I know about building certain kinds of little hand-props, which has helped once or twice, especially with David's more esoteric projects. Studying stage-fencing was useful for one particular piece that — no, you can just speculate on it.

But what fascinated me most was watching the directors at work. When a director bitched at someone about not delivering a line correctly I sort of tuned it out, because I could never hear much difference between what the director liked and what he didn't. But I loved to watch him do the blocking.

You've got this stage — a three-dimensional space — and you have people and sets and props, and you not only have to show the action such that the whole audience can see it, but you have to make it visually interesting the whole time, even when the models, er, actors are standing there talking. If everyone was moving all the time it would be like dance, but it isn't. Think about getting people to set themselves into positions where they can not only be seen, but the total tableau looks interesting, and remember that they usually have the blocking done after the sets are defined but before they're actually ready. Talk about a composition problem! Sheesh.

Doing this for proscenium is bad enough (though I'd love the chance!) but the idea of a thrust stage (or a round one) boggles the mind. I won't live that long. But I think I learned something about use of space.

3. *Tahitian Girls Bearing Mango Blossoms*

I hate it when someone is mad at me. Even when it's someone I don't like, just the notion that there's someone walking around cursing and fuming about something I did makes me queasy — sick to my stomach. I hate it. It's much, much worse when it's someone I care about. And Karen does really matter to me.

I skipped training on Thursday and almost didn't go in to the studio at all, but I finally showed up around nine in the evening. Robert and David were there. I said, "Howdy, guys."

"Lo, Greg," said David. Robert gave me an absent nod from upstairs.

I said to David, "Hey, do you know if Karen is still pissed at me?"

"No, I don't," he said. "She wasn't in today."

"Oh. Great."

I went up the stairs to Robert, still thinking too much, then said, "You seen Karen today?"

"No."

"Talked to her?"

He shook his head.

I said, "Oh."

I stood behind him. He was doodling. He drew a rectangle, then put a cross in it, then another one diagonally. He filled in every other one of the eight sections, saw that it was turning into an iron cross, scratched it out and looked up at me. "I like where you're going with the

Monster. It's good stuff. Keep at it."

I said, "Thanks. Look, I'm sorry about the whole thing with Karen. I —"

"Yeah. I'm sorry, too. I shouldn't have pushed you into it."

"I —"

"Maybe Dan is right, you know?"

"About the studio? About there not being any point in it?"

He nodded. I looked around. The view from up there is different. I'd noticed that before. The ceiling is only eight feet or so over your head, instead of twenty, so it feels cramped in comparison. And looking out over the rest of the studio makes you feel like you're observing the rest of us, instead of being part of the whole thing. Maybe that accounts for Dan's attitude, and Robert's.

Not that I really think so.

"I don't think it matters," I said.

"What do you mean?"

"We don't have any money for a show, we're at each other's throats to the point where we can hardly say three words to each other, and it doesn't seem to be getting any better. It's probably going to fall apart on its own."

Robert said, "That's what I've been thinking."

I stood there for a moment, but there didn't seem to be anything else to say. I stopped to take a quick look at "Lost" on my way back to work. I stopped indeed, stared, turned back to Robert and said, "What the fuck?"

"Huh? Oh, Dan's started a new project."

"But he wasn't finished with the last one."

"Yeah, well, he decided to put it aside."

"Put it aside?" Dan never put a painting aside until it was done. Down below, against the back wall, were about twenty billion old canvases. We'd started with five stacks, one for each of us, and that had lasted about three days. Now there must have been over a hundred paintings there, several of them thirty-six by thirty, which was what Dan's been using.

One of them was, "Lost," by Daniel Stoddard, unfinished, stuck back amid my failures and Karen's successes and David's experiments. Un-fucking-finished.

I studied the new canvas on his easel, my eye following the light sketch marks. I saw a river cutting the painting in half, upper right to lower left, a couple of little bodies looking like corpses even with the light sketching, and a field, maybe a soccer field, with the tiny circles of the type Dan uses to mean, "Put in J. Random Figure about this size." Dominating the lower right was a building complex. I'm not real up on current events, but I do know a nuclear reactor when I see one.

I turned to Robert again. "Have you seen this?" My voice was hoarse.

"What? Oh, yeah. I guess Dan was upset by Chern — Cheren — whatever it is. That place in Russia."

"He's doing anti-nuke stuff? Dan is doing anti fucking nuclear paintings?"

"Yeah. What's wrong with that? You pro-nuke?" He seemed only faintly curious; not especially interested.

"Huh? I don't know. But why is he doing this? Jesus Christ, he's gotten on a goddamn bandwagon, and he's going to give up art to —"

"Hey, maybe he cares about nuclear waste and all that."

I shook my head but I couldn't manage to speak. I needed Dan to be there so I could shake him, and I was glad he wasn't because I would have. The most beautiful painting in the goddamn world and he just *stops* to do this thing that everyone who was anti-nuke would agree with anyway, and everyone who was pro-nuke would hate on sight, and none of them would fucking *look* at to begin with.

I heard a growling sound and realized I was making

it. I decided I'd better get over to my easel before I took a knife to Dan's canvas.

4. *The Isle of the Dead*

There's a brush in my hand, and the colors are dark, perhaps red, and I attack the ground below Uranus. Then I move up. I cut him. He's dead, right? No, better, how about dying? That way he can bleed. Yeah, let it run down to the center. Let it hurt.

Make it hurt.

More colors built, the brush is small, the strokes choppy, and I etch pain onto his face. He didn't die happy. Take that, Dan.

Dan.

Why did you do that? You're the best fucking artist I've ever met. I've been trying to get a bloody day-job so you could keep working.

Red slashes across the sky, deep, hard, fading out and washing away, blending with endless night. A diagonal cut, tracing into an arc ending, almost vanishing before the mountain, the other end points to a dying god. A reverse rainbow — a rainbow of rage, a rainbow of betrayal.

God damn motherfucker. I don't know if I shout it out loud, and I don't care. No, a bigger brush. The small one flies across the room, still wet with paint. Maybe I'll wreck the carpet. Maybe I'll do a stain that will be considered a masterpiece someday. Where's the quarter-inch? All right, none of this bright shit. Black and grey, black and grey, black and grey. Wide strokes around the gate, isolate it, tie it to the wolf, who killed Uranus, but he's still hungry, get it? Good joke, huh?

How could he do that to me?

More red, now. Touch the black into it. More black, darker, darker, darker. Thank you, Dan, you've found the hate in me. Now you can see it. Admire your handiwork, you son-of-a-bitch.

And the hours fly by like the vultures of Dis.

5. *Sheep*

The old hag is still riding toward them, and look! Csucskári is standing, frightened. But then, suddenly, he sees a cottage not too far away.

"Come brothers," he says. "We must try to find shelter in that cottage. Perhaps it will be safe."

So they run for the cottage. Just in the nick of time, they make it to the cottage and shut the door in the hag's face. Meanwhile, she begins circling the cottage, waiting for them to come out.

The cottage was a blacksmith's shop, and the blacksmith was there. Csucskári said, "Sir blacksmith, we are being chased by an old hag. If you can save us, we'll give you anything we have."

"Well, I can save you," says the blacksmith, "but in return, you must swear to serve me for the rest of your lives."

So, having no choice, Csucskári and his brothers swear to serve the blacksmith for the rest of their lives.

6. *Hope*

Somebody said, if you can't hate, then you can't love. Well, I don't know. I'm suspicious of things you can say that easily, but it might be true. It might be true for me, anyway. If the part of me where hate can live is empty, that's fine, but if I didn't have that part, I wouldn't be able to feel pain, and what's love without pain?

That's what Karen can't understand. No, you don't have to go around showing ugly all the time. But for there to be pretty, there has to *be* ugly, doesn't there? The challenge isn't to show ugly, any more than it is to show pretty. There may be people out there who need to see that ugliness exists, but I'm not interested in talking to them. I know there are people out there who've never seen beauty, and I want to reach them, and say, "Hey, look, it's right in front of you."

You can't do that if you cut yourself off from the ugly. You have to see it all, or you can't understand any of it, and beauty without understanding is a pretty shallow thing after all.

Oh, I've met some of those guys who say, "Hey, I'm tough, I can deal with ugly." Crap. The goal is beauty, and ugly is what you pass through to find it. If you pretend it isn't there, you aren't showing anything. If you only look at the ugly, you aren't showing anything worth seeing.

Beauty that's on the surface is meaningless. Ugliness underneath is only the first stop. You have to work to find the real beauty, but it's there.

God knows, it's there.

Bones?

CHAPTER
·FIFTEEN·

1. *THE CIRCUS*

ONE DAY DURING my sophomore year a few
friends and I went to the coffee house under the Union,
where they had some decent acts every once in a while.
This time we didn't know the performer, we just felt like
going. I was with a girl named Sharon. She was taller
than I and had fantastic red hair, wonderful, deep green
eyes, and was just breaking a habit of acting stupid.

I'm not going to name the guy who was on stage
because he's still around. We were sitting in back when he

came on — a skinny white guy with a beat-up looking guitar. He sat down in front of the mike, adjusted it, tuned a bit, and said, "Ah's gwan t' sing da bal-ooze."

If it hadn't been for Sharon's presence, I would have walked out. We ended up staying, and he really wasn't that bad, but my god! "Ah's gwan t' sing da bal-ooze"!

I've forgiven him since then. I eventually realized he wasn't any older than I was, and was trying just as hard as I was, and I ought to give him a break. I've seen him once or twice since, and he doesn't do that sort of thing any more.

But for as long as I can remember I've hated phonies. I spent a long time being one myself; pretending to be macho; or pretending to be a super-sensitive, "caring" type; or pretending to be the deep, introspective artist; or any of a number of things. Since we're being honest today, I'll have to say that I haven't stopped, either. I still try to be things, maybe in the hopes that one of them will stick. One result of playing all those games, though, is that I've got almost no patience for other people who do, and I can spot them easily. You may call this hypocritical if you want to, and I can't argue, but there it is. Just thought you should know.

2. *A Summer Night*

The thing about Beethoven's music is its inevitability. The next note is always required by logical necessity from all those that lead up to it — required, predetermined, yet still an accomplishment, exciting in its realization.

I had a revelation while Debbie and I were listening to Toscanini conducting the NBC Orchestra doing Beethoven's Third in a 1953 recording. Many revelations have occurred to me while listening to the Eroica; it's that sort of piece. When I listen to it straight, as I was this time, some of the revelations are occasionally worth something.

I was trying to understand what it was that I liked about it, and what it had in common with other music I like. That is, why music hits me, and in particular, why some music does and some doesn't. Let's ignore the difference between "music" and "song" for the moment, as well as the difference between liking a composer and liking a performer. Tell me why I so enjoy my secret vice, Led Zeppelin, whom everyone else despises or has forgotten? Why do I flip out for Billie Holiday, but not Tchaikovsky? Why Mozart but not Steeleye Span? What is it that makes music work for someone but not for someone else?

I didn't get anywhere at all with that question, but something else hit me while I was trying to figure it out. I was noticing the particular beauty that Beethoven has, the inevitability of each sequence. I had almost decided I had something when, during the funeral march, he pulled a fast one — changed gears, as it were. There's this spot where the first violins are straining up at this high note, and, just as they stop, the basses and cellos come in on the same note a few octaves down, and then the trumpets and the horns come in like a musical landslide and blow you away. It seems completely disconnected from the rest of the piece; in fact, it threw me so hard it was almost a physical jolt, and I felt lost. But then the theme came back and picked me up and I knew that he'd been in control from the beginning; in fact, that he couldn't possibly have done it any other way.

The jolt, that's what I realized. You *want* that jolt. Later that evening I put on "Flute Thing" by The Blues Project, and I caught the same thing happening. Just at the point where they've wandered so far out that you think they'll never make it home, the theme comes back in and you realize it had never left.

That's what does it — that moment where you think you're lost, and then discover that you're not, that you've never really left. There's something that happens in that incredible tiny no-time, and that something is like the revelation of learning.

No, this didn't answer the question that I'd been asking, but it gave me a handle on one of the things about Dan's work that I've always loved, and on my own that I've tried to get without being aware of it. As the eye follows the lines into the center of focus, there is, almost unnoticed, a little splash of color, really the last thing you see, that almost doesn't belong. But it *does* belong, and puts a new perspective on the entire work, and *that's* what I'm always after — to create that *moment*, that empty space of time, where something, for want of a better word, *develops* in the mind of the viewer, and, perhaps, his world is changed.

3. *Skeletons Around a Stove*

I walked into the studio about two o'clock on Friday. I'd had time to think about things, and it hadn't helped much. I went straight up to Dan, who was applying paint to that thing on his easel. There was no sign of anyone else in the place, which was just as well.

I said, "What are you doing?"

He said, "What? Oh. A new project."

I said, "Why?"

He said, "Huh?"

I said, "Why did you stop working on the other one? It was great."

He seemed puzzled, from which I deduced that he hadn't spoken to Robert. "I don't know. I guess this hit me, so I decided to do it. If we're going to do the show, I want this one in it."

I didn't tell him just how likely I thought the show was. Instead I said, "But it's *junk*."

He looked at me.

I said, "That isn't art. That's just talking to hear yourself speak."

He said, "What are you talking about? It isn't even done yet."

I said, "I can see the sketch, can't I? It's your basic anti-nuclear horse-puckey."

He said, "Are you in favor of nuclear power? Even now, after we've seen —"

"I don't know. I haven't thought about it that much. The point is —"

"You haven't thought about it? You haven't *thought* about it? The whole world almost ended last week, and you haven't even *thought* about it?"

"What I've thought about is that you could be one of the greatest artists who ever —"

"I'll tell you what. Why don't you think about it. Then we can talk about what is and isn't important, all right?"

"I don't give a shit what's important. How do you want people to look at that, anyway? What do you want them to feel?"

"If they feel anything at all, it may get them thinking about it. Doesn't that matter?"

"What are you going to do next, Dan? Going to put a morality play on canvas? Don't you think their immortal souls are important? Or maybe you could do something on —"

"Just kill it, all right? If you don't like it, you don't have to look at it."

"Like I said before, horse-puckey. We're trying to do something —"

"Don't talk about what *we* are trying to do. This is what *I'm* trying to do."

"And I think it's wrong. I think you're taking all your skill and flushing it —"

Dan was staring over my shoulder. I turned around,

and Robert was upstairs walking over to us. It says something that I hadn't heard him on the way up. He didn't look happy. He was looking at me. He had something in his hand. He stopped about two feet in front of me and threw it down on the floor. I looked at it, and saw a twenty dollar bill, a ten, and a bunch of denominations I couldn't see.

I said, "What's that?"

He said, "Five hundred bucks."

I said, "You're kidding. Where did you get that?"

"For my bike."

It took a second to penetrate. "Your bike? You sold your bike?"

"Yeah. I took the bus here."

"For Chrissake why?"

"Don't be an asshole, Greg. You told me to, didn't you?"

"I *what?*" I suddenly wondered if I were in a dream. I looked about the studio. It all *seemed* real, but it does in dreams, too. I've had dreams where I wondered if I were dreaming. But no, this was real.

Robert sat down in his chair and said, "When you made that crack about David's Harley I knew what you were saying. So I sold it. Now we can do the show, and —"

"Robert, you don't even *own* a fucking Harley. And five hundred isn't enough to do the show anyway."

"You want me to raise all of it by myself?"

"Rob, I was *joking*. Funny. You know, ha-ha? Laugh? I wasn't trying to tell you —"

"Sure."

I stared back and forth between Dan and Robert. They were both looking at me. There's a point where anything you say is just going to make matters worse, and I decided that I was at that point. I wanted to run out of the studio and find a taxi to jump in front of. Instead, as calmly as I could, I turned and walked back to the Monster, trying to ignore the depression that seemed about to overwhelm me. I got out my paints.

4. *The Scream*

My movements felt tight and controlled as I mixed the flesh-tones and darkened them a bit. I found a small brush and diddled with Uranus's face. I decided I wasn't satisfied with his expression. I pretty much wiped out all his features and started over, making his eyes a little wider than I had before, and his face a bit less contorted, with stronger features.

I dealt with his face in tiny little strokes, a thin coating of paint. Everything was so clear, so precise. It scared me a bit. I'd never felt anything like that.

I drew pain on his features, death agony, and I thought about the three years we'd put into this place, and the more than three years of friendship. Had the gods in the painting been friends before this? Maybe. I wondered, would Apollo and Artemis ever be friends again?

I lightened some brown with a bit of white and some yellow, then did the lines around Artemis's eyes, then, with my smallest brush, did her pupils, in black. I used the brown to do the lines on her brow over again, lightening the color just a bit more with each successive line.

This was a room I didn't like being in, but I could work from here. The little man was pulling the strings and twisting the knobs, but he wasn't enjoying it.

I still had the funny brown, so I used it to suggest shadows in Artemis's arm and shoulder. When I'd finished that, a glance told me that Uranus's face wasn't quite done, so I worked more on his expression. I didn't want the agony of physical pain, I wanted the agony of understanding mortality, which made him human, and real. I touched up his lips, drawn back a bit so he was grimacing instead of snarling.

The gentlest touch of gloss covered the pupil of one dark eye, then a little more, until, if you looked really close, you might detect a tear, shed in lamentation of the earth he was losing and the friends who had betrayed him.

5. *Cardplayers*

The old hag with the iron nose (I forgot to mention, she had an iron nose) rode up on her shovel. She came to the door and called out, "Hey, my friend, didn't Csucskári and his two brothers come here?"

The blacksmith winks at Csucskári then calls out past the door, "So he did, mother."

"Then you must give them to me at once. He has killed my three sons. Three champions they were, and you would not find their equal, not in seven counties."

The blacksmith winks at Csucskári again, then says, "Oh, mother, you'd better forget about it. It's not so simple at all with a fellow like Csucskári. If I were to give him to you through the window, he might run away; if I were to give him to you through the door, he might knock you off your feet and get away. Why, there's no way of getting him to you unless I cut a hole in my wall and push him straight into your mouth."

"Well, then," says the hag. "That is what you shall do."

"Oh, but mother, will you repair my wall?"

"If you cut a hole in it and push Csucskári through, then I will repair your wall after I have eaten him."

"Very good then, mother. I will cut a hole in this wall and push him through. You must stand there and catch him in your mouth. Then you can bite him into pieces."

Well, as quick as lightning, the smith takes a pot big

enough to hold sixty quarts and starts to boil some lead in it. When the lead was melted, Csucskári took hold of the pot while the blacksmith cut a hole in the wall. When the hole was cut, the blacksmith called out, "Hey, mother! You'd better put your mouth close up to the hole so that not even an inch of Csucskári may slip past it, or he might get away."

"Well," says the hag, "I'm ready. Push Csucskári through the hole."

As soon as she says this, Csucskári pours all sixty quarts of lead through the hole. Then they go rushing outside, and the hag with the iron nose lay dead as a doornail.

"Thank you," says Csucskári. "We owe you our lives."

"Well," says the blacksmith, "and you shall repay me, too. Don't you remember that you have promised to serve me for the rest of your life? And don't think to fool me, either, for this is what I can do." And with that, he took a manikin and tied it into three hundred and sixty-six knots.

6. Crows Over the Cornfields

There is something that it has taken me quite a while to realize. I figured out a long time ago that if something is too easy, it probably isn't very good. But just because something is difficult doesn't mean that it's worth anything.

I know artists who spend their lives trying to find something to say that's never been said before. Others spend their time doing things that have been done and done again; repeating themselves and others. Still others look at art as if it were its own universe, and content themselves with pointing things out about their universe as if nothing else mattered.

As for the first, you say what you have to say the best way you know how, and that's it. Digging around in the dirt of ideology looking for a statement like a bird grubbing for worms is not my idea of how to create art.

Doing the same thing over and over again probably makes sense if someone is paying you for it and that's all you're interested in, but I can't really see it. You work on improving your technique and, sooner or later, you find you have to grow. Then you accept the challenge, or you don't. If you don't, well, I hope you make some bucks, at least.

And as for those who think of art as existing in its own universe, as if it has no relationship to life, I have nothing but contempt for them. If you have to be an art expert to understand and appreciate what I've done, then what I've done doesn't have a lot of value. Sure, whoever wants to look at your painting ought to do some work, but it's up to you to make him want to; to do a painting that asks to be looked at.

We all dream of doing something with lasting value —something that will outlive us. I mean, immortality is the name of the game, right? But you can't control that. What you *can* control is whether you do something that has some meaning to people who are alive today. An artist can't afford tunnel vision. If all you see is art, the only people your work will address are artists, and you might as well be blind.

When all is said and done, it may turn out that I have no real gift. It may turn out that I have nothing to say. It may turn out that I'm so wrong-headed I might as well not bother.

But give me one thing: I'm not blind.

Bones?

CHAPTER ·SIXTEEN·

1. *THE BLINDMAN*

IT COMES BACK as fragments, now.

The time I brought my bass over, and Karen had her guitar, and David had the backs of paint brushes to play on boxes and empty coffee cans. The studio was filled with people. Debbie was there, Robert's then-girl-friend, Mr. Winters, Phil, who owns the building we're in and seems fascinated by us. We all got drunk and sang Beatles tunes for hours. Dan wasn't there, as I recall.

There was the time Robert scored some magic mushrooms, and the bunch of us wandered around the place studying the walls of the studio and the decorations and cartoons and dissolving into hysterical laughter about every ten minutes. Come to think of it, Dan wasn't there then, either.

Robert has a friend named Curt who does magic shows, and one time they came by with about eight or nine people, walked into the middle of the place with no warning, set up, and did an hour-long show. Karen squealed like a nine-year-old, and David just watched with his mouth hanging open. Dan may have been there that time; I can't remember.

And all of the late, late-night talks, when you're not stoned, but you're so tired you might as well be, when you just sit there glowing with warmth, and all of those things that you really hope for come out, and you connect with each other on such deep levels that, when you think about it the next day, you wonder if it was real — if the others felt it too.

Come to think of it, I don't think Dan was around for any of those, either.

2. *The Mexican War of Independence*

David and I once finished pieces at just about the same time. The whole rest of the day we spent hearing what was wrong with our canvases (from each other, too, which completed the irony) until we were both near tears. We were the last two in the place that night, and as we were sitting there trying to decide whether to get stoned David said, "Hey, Greg, with all the pain this causes me, why do we do it?"

I didn't have an answer, of course. I still don't.

I think, taken as a whole, painting causes more pain than pleasure for the artist. No, I'll go further than that: Any art causes more pain than pleasure for the artist.

Don't get me wrong; I don't want to come at you with this horrible, oh, woe is me, poor struggling artist suffering for his vision crap, but, adding it all up, it does hurt; often and a lot.

I think one reason that I've gotten so down on certain kinds of critics is because that way I get to sniff the air and turn away when they look at work I love and tell me, "That isn't art, that's illustration." I get down on them because, when they say that, it hurts.

If sometimes I rant and rave about how *only* what I'm doing is legit, that's partly because it puts me in a strong position for feeling I'm doing real art. When someone I care about says, "You're not bad, why aren't you doing *serious* art?" it hurts.

I don't show my work as, well, aggressively as I might, because when someone I've never met looks at one of my paintings, smiles politely and moves on, it hurts.

I wear biker leathers and study karate because when I run into someone who thinks artists must be wimps, it hurts.

When I think about everything Debbie could have for herself if she weren't supporting me, it hurts.

When Robert and David and Karen and Dan go, "Yeah, that's nice," and then spend half an hour pointing out what's wrong with it, hell, I know why they're doing it, it's for the same reason I do when I'm looking at one of their works. But, God damn it, it *hurts*.

I could go on, but what's the point? There are good times, when the guys in the studio say, "Yeah, Greg, that's good," it feels really nice. When Debbie says it, it feels really nice. When someone I've never met says it, and means it, it's wonderful. But somehow it's the pain that sticks in my memory.

So why do I do it?

I don't know. I just do. A rose is a rose, and an artist is an artist. It doesn't mean I'm good; it's just what I do.

If I end up getting a job as a draftsman, I'll be miserable. I know that now.

But, of course, that's no guarantee that I won't have to anyway. In fact, it looks pretty likely. When those to whom you habitually turn for support aren't there — mostly because you've offended them — well, that's a new kind of pain. And when I trace the causes back far enough, it turns out that I had thought we all held pretty much the same opinions on what is and isn't good art. Now I find that I'm in a minority of one, and, no matter how firmly I believe what I believe, it shakes me up.

As a human being, I have Debbie to lean on, and I'm grateful. But now I wonder what I have to lean on as an artist. I've always been depending on my own ideas, and the people who share them, and nature itself. Now it seems like these people are out to make me question my ideas of nature.

Why would they want to do that?

But, hell, I'll be a *good* draftsman.

3. *Premonition of Civil War*

I slunk into the studio just after noon. Robert and Dan were both in, and Dan was working. I got a cup of coffee and took a long time doctoring it. After a while I realized I was looking for patterns in the whirlpool of coffee, fake cream, and sugar stirred up by the red swizzle stick.

I walked back into the studio proper and made my way over to the Monster. I knew Robert must be really down; he had Dire Straits going on the tape player and Dan hadn't asked him to kill the noise.

I sat down on the fluffy, gray cushions I keep for models. Robert caught my eye then looked away. Dan kept working. I could see the back of his neck and head, and I was willing to bet he was clenching his teeth. He'd set up his lights by himself this time, and they were coming from the side so I was getting a bit of a glare, and the bit of Dan's face that I could see when he turned his head was mostly in shadows, with one bright eye glowing. His brows stick out quite a way from his head. I'd never noticed that before.

I stood in front of my easel and thought about working, changed my mind, sat down again and drank more coffee. A couple of times I slurped too loudly and Robert turned to look at me, started to say something but didn't. I wished to hell he had.

Dan put down his brushes and came down and sat next to me. Neither one of us spoke for a while. The scene suddenly reminded me of when I had broken up with Joanne, just after leaving college. I said, "I only want what's best for both of us."

Dan said, "What?"

I said, "Never mind. Private joke."

He said, "I think this is probably it for the studio, you know."

I said, "I know. I've really blown it, haven't I, what with one thing and another?"

He said, "I don't think it's you. I think it just came up that way. We've served our purpose, and I don't think there was anything more the studio had to offer us."

"Hey, Dan, why is it that whenever you decide to do something, you have to come up with three volumes of Hegelian philosophy to explain it?"

He started to argue, but then changed his mind and shrugged. He lay back against the cushions and put his arm over his eyes. He was still lying there when Karen came charging in like a buffalo stampede.

Karen is almost as good at concealing things as I am; which is to say not at all. I took one look at her face, got up, and walked over to her. Robert turned the tape off and came down.

I said, "Congratulations."

She said, "It shows, huh?"

I said, "Yeah. Which one, to whom, and for how much, or how tall is he?"

She laughed. "Which ones, not which one."

I said, "Which *ones?* Christ on a Ferris wheel. Tell me about it. "

Dan had come over, too, and Robert took Karen's arm and started beaming.

" 'Flower Arrangement,' thirty percent, Midway Galleries."

"*Midway Galleries?* You're kidding. They're hanging it? That's great."

"And when I was talking to Jessie, there —"

"Jessie?"

"The owner of the gallery. There was a guy looking over my shoulder who just flat out bought 'Jay's Nest.' "

Robert hugged her. I said, "That's wonderful. We need to throw a party."

"Not a party. A show. I got two hundred and fifty for it. With what Robert got for his bike, that's enough to do it if we squeeze. We can probably come up with a little more if we have to."

Dan said, "Tell me about it."

Robert let go of her and they both plopped down on the beanbags next to Robert's table.

She said, "I just called up last week, asked the manager if I could bring in a portfolio, brought it in, she liked some of the pieces. She said to bring in some canvases. So today I brought about six of them to the gallery and she hung the flower arrangement. She said she'd hang more later if that one sold. And then there was this other guy." She laughed. "He *made* me take his name down when I said we might be doing a show."

I shook my head. "That's great, Karen." As I said it, it sounded kind of hollow, although no one else seemed to notice. I backed up a step. *What's wrong with me?* I knew I couldn't actually be jealous just because Karen sold a painting and had another one hung in a gallery.

Could I?

Sure I could.

It was there all right. A cold hard knot, something I'd never thought I'd be capable of. Of all the revolting things to feel, that had to take it.

I wondered if I was going to throw up. But there it was, in the back of my brain, thoughts like, why did it have to be Karen? *Any* of the rest of us. Why not one of Robert's pen and inks? Why not something of Dan's? Why Karen?

What an ugly, ugly, way of looking at it. That was the worst part. Karen had picked up a bottle of champagne along the way and had it chilled. I toasted her and went back to stand in front of The Monster for a while, trying to make myself feel happy for Karen.

Pretty soon Dan came over. "Problem?" he said.

"Yeah. I think you've sold me too well."

"You don't want to do the show?"

"You got it."

"You sound really upset."

I looked at him. "I *am* really upset."

"About Karen?"

"That's part of it. More of it's being upset that I'm upset. But look, Dan. Let's be honest, all right? Robert is pissed as hell at me because he thinks I made him sell his bike. I can't stand the work you've started, and you're pissed at me because of that. Karen knows what I think of her work, and is pissed because of that, and I'm jealous of her selling and hate myself for it. David has almost stopped working completely.

"I don't know if I'm down on doing the show or not, but I don't think I fit in here any more. It's senseless. I think I ought to just pack up and split, and you guys can keep going without me."

Dan was quiet for a while, then he said, "I really

don't think we'll have a studio without you."

"Manure," I suggested.

He shook his head. "No. You're the one who provides the enthusiasm."

"Yeah. Well, I'm doing a great job of it, aren't I?"

Dan said. "Let's think about the show some more. I don't know. Maybe we can do it one time before we dissolve. If we get lucky, some of us might get a break or two for afterwards."

"Then you agree with me? About giving up the studio?"

He nodded.

"Shit," I said.

He nodded and went back to tell Karen and Robert. I stood there with my back to them. I heard voices raised, but tuned out any bits of conversation I heard. Then they dropped their voices and went upstairs, either so they could bitch about me more comfortably or maybe because they thought I was working and didn't want to disturb me.

Since I preferred the latter, I pretended to work for a while. Eventually David came over. He just stood next to me.

I said, "All right, David. What do you do when you start questioning everything you've ever believed about art?"

He was still for the space of three breaths; when he spoke, he sounded the way I do when I'm trying to get every word exactly right so as not to say the wrong thing. He said, "It may be that you're overstating things."

"I don't think so," I said. "When I try to figure out why it is I've offended so many of my friends, I have to decide that either I'm a worthless human being, or we're bumping into differences in our opinions on art that I hadn't known were there. Or maybe that I just ignored. I'd rather not consider myself a worthless human being.

Of course," I said, almost smiling, "it could be all my opinions on art are just wrong. Naw, couldn't be."

He didn't say anything. I stared at the Monster.

A bit later I said, "It doesn't really matter any more, though, does it?"

"I suppose not."

I took another breath or two. "David?"

"Yeah?"

"What am I doing wrong?"

He didn't answer, I looked at him. He seemed miserable. He met my eyes and said, "I wish you hadn't asked me that."

I started to say, "I withdraw the question," but then I changed my mind. Might as well satisfy all my masochistic urges at once.

He said, "You're too cocky."

Cocky? I said, "Cocky?"

"Yeah. You have all these theories, and that's fine, and you're probably right more than you're wrong. But once you've answered something, you stop looking."

"I don't understand."

He sighed. "All right, you know how we say you have to keep developing as an artist? Well, if you're going to try to be a — what's the word? I don't know, a theorist, maybe. If you're going to be a theorist as well, you have to keep developing that way, too. You can't be content with easy answers any more than you can be content with the paintings that are easy to do. Does that make sense?"

I said, "I guess so. But, shit, man. Where am I wrong?"

"Hell, I don't know. I'm not trying to be a theorist. Besides, I agree with all your theories anyway."

I looked at him again. There was a bit of a smile about his lips. For the first time in my life, I regretted that my urges were so completely heterosexual, because part of me wanted to make love with him right then. I wonder if he felt any of that.

I turned back to my canvas. Misery mitigated, but misery still.

What a bitch.

4. *Echo of a Scream*

I was feeling distinctly uninspired, but there were details I hadn't yet attended to. Like dressing poor Artemis. I wanted something cold (the color, not the outfit), like a blue, only I couldn't see Artemis in anything except earth tones. Well, okay, what do you want? Realism or expressionism? I chuckled to myself at the question.

Then I built up a pale beige, tested it on a piece of canvas on the table and decided it matched my mood pretty well. Aside from that, it might work for the painting.

I laid it down over Artemis, not like a dress, but more like an undergarment; something between her skin and the clothing I'd do next. It was so subtle as to be almost invisible in how it matched her skin tones, but I thought it might do the job.

What do you feel when pale, sickly, watery blue matches your mood?

Why, nothing. Nothing at all.

I gave Artemis a short, tight garment that wouldn't interfere with running, or be easily caught on brambles, yet was feminine. This was a classical subject — sort of — so she had to dress like a she.

I took another look at Apollo and thought about the battle he'd been through. It was tricky because of all the coats of gloss I'd put over but I was able to throw in some indications that he, too, had been in a fight. I gave him a tiny wound on his cheek, and a cut on his leg. No great amounts of blood; just a suggestion.

I decided I liked the way the blood-red worked against the highlighted, glossy flesh. Even though the wounds didn't stand out too much, they gave the feeling they didn't belong there, like, "No! Not Apollo. He *can't* be hurt." If someone caught that, he would think I'd done it deliberately, and I sure wasn't going to enlighten him.

Just for the hell of it, I put a nasty gash across the wolf's hide. Why should he have been left out? I told Uranus. "There. You gave them a good fight. Feel better now?"

His face still expressed the pain of loss. Fighting the good fight, I guess, didn't mean much to him.

On a whim, I put one of Artemis's, or perhaps Apollo's arrows into his side. Then I caught myself. His side? Oh, Lord, someone's going to go, "Christ-figure, Christ-figure," which wasn't at all what I had in mind.

I think.

I glanced at his hands and feet to make sure my subconscious hadn't done anything to them I'd regret later.

His right hand, though unwounded, held a trace of the blood from his chest. Right in the God damn palm. I didn't know whether to laugh or to cry.

I built up the flesh tone that I'd used for Uranus and darkened it a bit, then I worked some of the blood into the details of his hand, and covered over most of the rest. I couldn't bring myself to cover it all. If my subconscious was so bound and determined to do this, I might as well let it have its way, but I didn't have to be so obvious, did I?

I left the arrow alone.

You want me to admit to how low I can go into the depths of revolting, maudlin self-pity? Okay, I will; it was only then that I realized that, for the last couple of days, I'd been identifying with Uranus.

Makes you sick, huh? I don't blame you.

5. *The Departure*

Time passed, and the brothers began to become anxious. Hadn't they gotten the box with the sun, the moon, and the stars in it? Weren't they ready to finish their task? But how could they escape from this blacksmith who could tie a manikin into three hundred and sixty-six knots?

The blacksmith had a wife. Soon Csucskári fell in love with her. So every day when he left the breakfast table he would bow to her in the manner of the gypsies. And every evening when he finished his work, he would wink at her in the manner of the gypsies. And every night before retiring to bed, he would blow her a kiss in the manner of the gypsies.

Well, soon she falls in love with him, too, and he wastes no time in asking her the secret of her husband's strength. How is it that he could move easily through hoops of steel, reaching up right to his knee, and by what trick could he tie up a man into three hundred and sixty-six knots? Well, his wife doesn't know, but she promises to find out.

At noon the blacksmith came home for his meal, and his wife said, "Oh dear and wonderful husband, I have been living with you for some thirty years now, but I have never asked you wherein lies that magnificent strength of yours."

At that the blacksmith fetched her such a blow in the face that she passed out for twenty-four hours. Next time she saw Csucskári, she said, "Oh, I tried to find out, but he struck me so hard I slept for twenty-four hours."

Csucskári said, "Never mind about that. If you ask him again, he'll tell you."

So the next day, she asked her husband again, "My dear husband, do tell me, pray, wherein lies your magnificent strength."

"Listen, wife. As you are so keen to find out, though

heaven only knows whether I shall not be sorry for it, I am willing to tell you. Look at that chain mail I always wear for a shirt. Without it, I possess no more strength than any other human being."

"Oh dear husband, if I had known it before, I would have had it gilded for you."

When the day turned to night and the smith went to sleep in his bed, his wife took off his shirt and gave it to Csucskári. At once Csucskári slipped into the shirt. Then he goes to his sleeping brother and ties him into three hundred and sixty-six knots to test the magic power of the shirt. Then he unties his brother.

Midnight came. The blacksmith wakes from sleep. At once Csucskári goes up to him. "Listen, brother smith. I am not going to serve you any longer."

Says the smith, "And why not, may I ask? Didn't you make a pledge that all three of you were to serve me as long as you live?"

"Indeed, we did, but that was some time ago."

"Just listen, brother. I know that all this is my wife's doing. I dare say, you have enough guts to oppose me, with tying up your brother, though you could not have done it without having taken my strength from me. But here you shall remain."

At this Csucskári seized the smith and tied him into three hundred and sixty-six knots.

"Oh, comrade, didn't I spare your life and your brothers' lives? Surely I may trust your kind heart and you will untie me before you leave this place."

Csucskári untied the smith and with his brothers took leave of him.

6. Night Cafe

What I want to emphasize is this: anytime an artist says, "The whole point of this piece is —" he's lying.

Sometimes it's crude and obvious. When someone

says, "That's supposed to be a garden? It doesn't look like a garden," and the artist says, "The whole point of this piece is to show you that a garden looks like a brick wall," your bullshit detector ought to go off.

I don't think I do that.

But sometimes it's harder. When people point out things in my work that they *like*, I've often heard myself saying, "Yeah. I'm glad you noticed that. The whole point of this piece is that she's more beautiful in his eyes than she is in the mirror, you know?" And then, on the same piece, a month later, "Yeah, I'm glad you noticed that. The whole point of this piece is that she can only find her self-worth from what he thinks of her, you know?"

I mean I'll catch myself at that sort of thing — and even worse examples that I won't torture myself by relating. I've heard other artists do it, too. I don't know why — I'm being completely honest every time.

So what really *is* the point? I don't know. I'm after something; I've been aware of that much for years. Not the same thing from piece to piece, you understand, but each time I start there is *something* that I'm trying to capture, and I never know quite what. I only know that, sometimes, I almost seem to get it. Once I painted a still life of fruit on a plate set against a backdrop of stars, almost as if it were floating in space, and that almost had it.

But not quite.

I haven't given up, though. And I'm not going to. Maybe this time it'll be there.

I suspect that when I finally do get it, whatever it is from this work or that, you'll know before I will.

Bones?

CHAPTER
•SEVENTEEN•

1. *SKULL AND ROSES*

IT WAS FUNNY running into Phil, my old college roommate. He'd aged a surprising amount in the four years since I'd seen him — say about as much as I had. He wasn't as tall as I'd remembered him, but he still had those bright blue eyes, and the rough, square face that always looked in need of shaving. And there were still all the memories. Like the collaborative water color we'd done of a baby who's head was much too small for his body, called "Child of the Renaissance."

We crossed paths in a coffee shop not far from the studio. He was wearing a navy blue three-piece suit. He told me what he was doing, and I said, "Jesus, Phil. It looks like you made it."

He laughed a bit. "I'm trying. How 'bout you?"

I said, "We've got a studio not far from here. You ought to stop in some time, see what we've been up to. Did you know Dan Stoddard?"

"Ummm, medium height, sandy hair, a little overbite, flat forehead, walked a bit hunched over?"

"Right."

"Never heard of him."

I laughed. "He's in it, too. He's doing some great stuff. You'd, like, die to see it."

He nodded absently. "How about you?" he asked.

"I'm doing the best I can, I guess. I'm still learning, but I think I'm on the right track."

"No, I meant, you know, personally. Where are you working?"

"I'm just doing art."

His eyebrows went up. "Is that right? You making anything off it?"

"Not yet. My girlfriend is kind of bankrolling me until things take off — if they ever do."

When I said that I could see him sort of shut down and close up. Like "disapproval" was written in the lines of his forehead. I felt really uncomfortable. Trying to recover, I said, "Hey, Phil, remember that big painting you did, back at the dorm, where you put an extra room in the place?"

He smiled. "Yeah. I was proud of that."

I nodded. "It was really something. You ever miss doing that sort of thing?"

"Not really. They keep me pretty busy."

"I guess. It's hard to imagine you not doing art, though."

He said, "You mean like that room thing? That isn't art. It's illustration."

2. *Portrait of Van Gogh*

I set up my easel and sculpt a tune of mixed metaphor.

Just in case it's escaped your attention, what I've been trying to do is understand the process of creation. It is something that has never failed to fascinate me. Think about it; all you have is some pigment and some linseed or poppy seed oil and some turpentine all mixed together, and you take a stick with some pig-hairs or something on it, and you use the latter to smear the former on a piece of canvas trying to say to anyone who sees it, "Feel joy. Feel pain. Feel delight. Feel sorrow. Feel comfort. Feel fear."

Absurd, no?

There are tricks to it, and they come in every flavor. If you use this color, it means warm and secure. If you shade this way, it will look more three dimensional. If you apply the paint in this fashion, you can use the tex- turing to convey what you want. And so on and on and on.

You take these tricks that we like to call "technique," and look around to see what you want to put on the can- vas, and decide how you want to do it, hoping to arouse some emotion on the part of the last, crucial element — the viewer. The whole thing continues to mystify me.

The tools are real. The viewer is real. You, the artist, are real and a part of everything you paint. You connect yourself to the viewer by sharing something that is inside of you that connects with something inside of him, using the vehicle of something you have seen which he can rec- ognize, and you show it in a way that presents it as some- thing he hasn't seen. All you have as your guide is that you know what moves you. All you have to do it with is a brush, some chemicals, a canvas, and technique.

You paint the sort of thing you like to see, and, when you think about it, hope the sort of thing you like to see can, somehow, be called, "good."

I know musicians who refer to technique as "chops" and I like that. All right. You spend your life practicing your chops with the brush to be able to make it do what you want, and training your eye to see what's there that means what you want, and, somehow, you transform these things into a painting that will move someone, perhaps to tears, and might, if he lets it, become a part of him, and so change his life.

It's all chops and taste.

3. *The Embrace*

I came in to the studio just to finish up the painting. Nothing else would have brought me there, but it was almost done, and, who knows? It might have been my best work. In any case I wanted to finish it. I didn't figure to start another for a while.

I was pleased to see that David was there, as was Dan, who was standing back from his canvas looking at it.

David said, "Howdy, Greg."

I said, "Yeah. Hi."

He said, "Pretty grim, huh?"

"Yeah. It's just that, I don't think I can work with any of these people. Except you, I guess. And who knows when we'll have a blow-up?"

He said, "Maybe we could, you know, get a place and do another studio, just us. That would be something anyway."

"Maybe. I don't know."

"Yeah, me neither. Look, for whatever it's worth, I don't think it's all your fault."

"No, not all my fault. Some of it is my mouth's fault.

If I could have keep it shut —"

He shrugged.

I said, "Maybe we could do another studio. It wouldn't be the same, though."

"No," he said. "It wouldn't."

After a moment I said, "I'm going to get to work."

"Yeah, okay. And, Greg, it looks really good. I think this is your best piece so far."

I said, "Thanks. That means a lot."

I looked up at Dan on my way toward the Monster. He still hadn't moved, and in fact wasn't holding his brushes. He turned as I walked by, then came down. I waited for him.

"You know," he said, "you're partly right."

I said, "I'm right about something? That's a switch. What about?"

He gestured up toward his canvas. "It is preaching to the converted. But you're wrong about the rest of it."

I shrugged. I didn't feel like arguing. We stood there for a moment, then he said, "I'm going to re-do it, I think. Make it a little less blatant."

I said, "You could finish 'Lost' first, you know."

"Maybe. Yeah, maybe I should." He looked at the canvas, then at me, as if I were modeling for him. "But you're still missing the point. There's no way you can say one is art and the other isn't."

I guess I just can't resist a good argument. "Sure I can," I said. "One is art and the other isn't."

"Why?"

"Because the job of art is to evoke emotion. It has to *mean* something to people, and that means people who are pro-nuclear power, anti-nuclear power, or don't know."

"You think it has to appeal to everyone?"

"No. But I don't think it can shut out anyone. That's the difference. It's like all those abstractionists, who are only going to appeal to people who are art experts anyway. You have to make them want to look at it. There should be some depth, some meaning, but first of all you have to make them want to look."

"You're a snob, Greg."

"Me? What are you talking about? My whole point is that —"

"I know. Art must be pleasing to the eye, so anyone can enjoy it, as well as containing enough depth —"

"That's right. I've said all that and I still agree with it. How does that make me a snob?"

"Because you say, 'art must.' "

I shrugged. "All right. Art can be anything. If I want to throw a pile of dirt at a wall full of glue, that's art. If I want to —"

"It can be," he said.

"Bullshit," I suggested.

"You always talk about 'art that's only for artists,' as if that disqualifies it. Well, so, there are people out there you just can't reach any other way, because they've seen too much art. Yeah, maybe they're a bit jaded; does that mean anything that appeals to them is automatically bad?"

I started to say, "Yes," but David's words came back to me. I didn't say anything.

Dan said, "You really ought to talk to Karen about art history sometime. You'd be surprised how many of those paintings that you like so much were created to play off the work of other painters. Check it out some time. The idea of art playing off what's already been done isn't new, Greg. It's been going on as long as there's been art."

I said, "All right, then, why is it that you don't function that way?"

"I do. When I first started thinking about 'Lost,' what I had in mind was putting Millet into the city.

Maybe it didn't come out that way, but so what?"

I thought it over. I didn't like it.

Dan said, "Look, okay, you aren't completely wrong. Yeah, I'd even agree that there's too little art being done today that deals with humanity. And, yeah, that's the sort of stuff that I want to do. But, Jesus, have you looked at Matta's work? Like 'Removal of the Cards'? It's fantastic. There's real beauty there, just with line and form and balance. You can't go around saying, 'Joe Blow won't get it, so it doesn't count.' You're a snob, Greg."

I blinked a couple of times, trying to find an answer, and I couldn't come up with one. After a moment he said, "That's the same trouble you have with Karen."

Huh? "Are you saying —?"

"I'm saying Karen's landscapes and horses are every bit as valid — "

"Valid. I hate that word. Valid. What the fuck does 'valid' mean, anyway?"

"To you? It means your kind of art, and that's all."

"But she isn't putting any —"

"She's putting into her work what she *wants* to put into it, which is just what you're doing. Maybe she isn't as pretentious as you, that's all."

That hurt. I turned my head away so Dan wouldn't see tears. After a moment he said, "Hey, I'm sorry. I didn't mean that."

I said, "Sure you did," trying for a light tone of voice. It didn't carry much conviction.

He said, "No I didn't. I respect what you're doing and why. And, yeah, what you do hits me a lot harder than what Karen is doing. It works for me. I think what you're doing with the Monster is really good, all right?"

"All right." My voice was hardly above a whisper.

"But all you really know is what you've been through. You don't know what Karen's been through, and neither do I. We know what she paints. She's finding beauty, and she's showing it to people who want to see it, and that's the bottom line. It just isn't your place to say that's wrong. With what's going on these days, it may be that the ability to see pure beauty is the most difficult thing there is, and that two hundred years from now she's going to be considered one of the great painters of the twentieth century. You can't know and neither can I. So just lighten up, okay?''

I said, "Yeah. Okay. It doesn't matter any more, does it? I mean, we're done, aren't we?"

He said, "The Monster is looking really good."

"Thanks."

"We really did help you on it, didn't we?"

"Yeah."

"I think you've helped me on this one. I mean, I might not have figured that out, about preaching to the converted, if you hadn't bitched at me."

I didn't say anything. I wondered if he were going where I thought he was going.

He said, "Do you understand what I was getting at about Karen?"

I said, "I think so."

He said, "Maybe we ought to reconsider."

I said, "Reconsidering, sir."

He said. "Let me think about it."

I stood there for a little longer, not knowing what else to do.

Dan said, "Yeah, I think I'll finish 'Lost.' " He went upstairs and took the canvas down from his easel and brought it back to the stacks.

I wandered back toward David and sat on his table. He said, "What was that all about?"

"Art appreciation, two-oh-oh-one."

"Sounds, um, educational."

"I guess."

Karen and Robert came in about then, arm in arm.

Robert was wearing his beret again. I said, "Hey, Karen."

"Yeah?"

"I'm sorry."

"For what?"

"Never mind. I just want to say I'm sorry."

"Ummmm, well, all right."

They continued back, and talked quietly with Dan for a while. David and I watched them without saying anything. Presently, Dan came over. "Wanna do the show, then?"

"Yeah," I said. David nodded.

Robert said, "I called up one of the art critics for *City Scene*, and he said he'd be there."

I said, "You're shitting me."

"Nope."

"Well, I'll be damned."

"Yep."

David said, "So, what about the studio? We can't stop now, can we? I mean, if we're actually going to get some attention, it's a really stupid time to quit."

Dan said, "Why don't we see what he says, first."

Robert said, "If he says anything at all, it'll be worth something. And this guy isn't blind, anyway. He might not like it, but if he does like it he has enough balls that he'll say so, and he'll at least admit we can paint, even if he doesn't like where we're going."

Karen said, "So, we're still in business?"

"Let's see what the critic says, first," said Dan, but he didn't have much heart in it.

I said, "Look, people, if we actually sell enough, can we agree that the first five hundred goes to replacing Robert's bike?"

"I'd go for that," said David.

"Me too," said Dan. "Hell, maybe a little more if we can, since it was selling the bike that got us going."

Karen didn't have to say anything — that was

obvious from the way she was holding Robert. I said,
"Gee, Unca Bobby, maybe you can even upgrade to a
decent bike."

He said, "Fuck you, Greg."

What a sweet thing for him to say. It warmed me all
over.

4. *The Rose*

I whistled as I dotted the last i's and crossed the last
t's. I'd have to go back and clean up; I was sure everyone
would have plenty of suggestions for me, but it was done,
and, all in all, I wasn't too unhappy with it. I'd found
my theme, at any rate. It wasn't something I could put
into words, but putting a theme into words isn't my job.

Somewhere amid the pain of dying and the pain of
killing and the triumph of opening a way, I felt a message of hope. Maybe that was my theme. But I knew it
was an honest work, and that was important. I knew that
it was almost done, and that was *very* important.

I touched up the shadows on the back of Apollo's
head, cleaned up a little sloppiness in Artemis's outfit,
touched up the rocks against which Uranus's head lay,
and darkened the base of the mountain. I added a last little bit of color, the final touch that defined the painting
and made it bright enough to attract the eye, signed it,
and put my paints away.

5. *Ghormenghast*

The brothers set off wandering, and after a while
Csucskári says, "My dear brothers, after all the trouble I
went through, let me take a little rest so that I may sleep
for a while."

Now since Csucskári was a *taltos,* he didn't need any
sleep. It was just that he wanted to test his brothers, to see

if they were loyal to him.

Said Holló, "Indeed, you deserve as much rest as you want. You sleep, and we'll keep watch."

Said Bagoly, "My dear brother Csucskári, you can make yourself comfortable when we have completed our mission and are at the king's palace. There you can take off your clothes and take a bath. That's where you should rest."

But Csucskári did not take heed of his words. There and then he lay down and soon was snoring away in sleep. Then Holló drew forth a razor and began to sharpen it. Bagoly said, "What are you doing, brother? Didn't you have a shave just last week? Surely you don't need another one now."

"I am going to cut Csucskári's throat, so that I may marry the king's daughter and get half his kingdom. Be quiet now, and I will share it with you, that way you'll get a quarter of the kingdom for yourself."

"And could you cut your brother's throat in cold blood knowing that it was Csucskári who did all the fighting and endured the many hardships? What else did we but follow him about, and surely that did not amount to much." And he called to the sleeper, "Wake up, my dear brother Csucskári! Our eldest brother is going to cut your throat."

Csucskári opened his eyes and said, "I knew it, my dear brother. I was not sleeping. It was only to test the true feelings of your hearts for me. But now you must disown our eldest brother and pledge yourself to have nothing to do with him, whatever state you may rise to in this world. He may not even hope to be taken on as a herdboy for your turkeys."

After that they took leave of Holló, and Csucskári and Bagoly came to the king's palace. There Csucskári said to the king, "Good day to you, sire. Your majesty, I have brought the sun and the moon and the stars for you but on the condition that you give your daughter in marriage and half of your kingdom to my brother and not to me because I am a *taltos*."

"That's all right by me," said the king.

Then they did justice to their agreement. Csucskári and Bagoly climbed to the top of Mount Szaniszlo. There Csucskári gave to Bagoly the shirt from the blacksmith, and Bagoly put it on so he could hold onto the River Tundar and make the earth stand still. Then Csucskári released the twelve wasps and the sun and the moon and the stars were fixed in the sky. And so there was light.

Throughout seven countries the drums went rolling and all the dukes and counts and great lords came together to celebrate the wedding. For seven years and seven winks the wedding feast went on.

And if they are not dead, they are still alive to this day.

6. *The Death of Uranus*

The painting is, perhaps, done. The studio is, perhaps, saved. The show will, perhaps, take place. It was a tough fight, ma, but — well, it was a tough fight.

Me? I'd like to think I learned something from all I've been through — painting the picture and everything else. I feel certain I did. But as to whether it was right or wrong, or good or bad, or assimilated or not, I guess I won't know for a while. That's all right. I'm feeling anxious to start another painting, but I'll have to wait. There are a few more coats of gloss to go on.

And you? I hope your eye travels the length of my canvas, stopping at the right places, and that you find something in there you like. I would be happy if you found in my painting something to make you say, "Hey, he's right; I hadn't noticed that." It would be nice if you were to find what I tried to put there, and even nicer if you discovered in the texture values of which I had no inkling.

Let your eye follow the lines, and look for the tiny splash of color that, oh so gently, redefines what you're looking at, so there is a flash or understanding, and you see the picture — or perhaps something of life — in a new way.

I most fervently hope, as your eyes follow the lines I so laboriously set, that you find at the end of the path that it has, for whatever reason, been worth the trip. And ultimately, it would be nice if you would find in my painting, in your own way and however you define it, something of beauty.

Merry meet again.

Kovacs '87

AFTERWORD
•THE ORIGIN OF FOLK BELIEFS•

What can properly be called scholarly studies into European folk beliefs originated only toward the latter second half of the 18th century. Goethe's somewhat older friend and colleague, the poet and literary critic of German Romanticism, Johann Gottfried Herder, was one of the major figures to begin and inspire others to continue a scientific investigation into the murky sources of folk literature.

As the outstanding contemporary Hungarian ethnologist, Tekla Domotor, has noted it is hardly an historical accident that interest in folk ways and culture co-incides with the formation of the modern nation states in Europe. It is also a period, she suggests, of the awakening of a lively curiosity by long oppressed minorities about their own national identity. Such fascination with one's ethnic roots clearly served political ends as well, particularly among the many nationalities under the jack boot of the Austrian Hapsburgs and the Czarist Romanoffs.

For the long-suffering Hungarians on the central European puszta as for so many other peoples concerned with securing national recognition, if not immediate independence, the research into their origins was seen by the politically motivated middle class students and scholars as a critical first step on the road to autonomy.

What astonished these earlier probers, just as it did other European toilers in the cultural vineyards, was the discovery that the supernatural, magic, animism, shamanism, fetishism, and many other cult beliefs associated with non-European primitive tribes were very much a part of the daily practice of the Magyar peasant as well, though far less true of his urban cousin.

On closer inspection it was revealed that a pervasive and uneasy co-existence prevailed in the largely Roman Catholic countryside between the outward observance of Christian rites on Sundays and holidays and a daily practice often quite antagonistic to the spirit and dogma of the Mother Church. It is an incredible tribute to the cunning of the Hungarian peasantry to have been able for almost a millennium to hang on so doggedly to their pagan ways without arousing the public wrath of Rome.

Of course, the papacy was hardly unaware of what existed through the centuries. But it chose to shut an eye to it all in preference to engaging in what would have been an open and unwinnable confrontation with so stubborn an adversary.

To be sure, this stubbornness in clinging to his ancient ways was not the result of some peculiarly national or psychological quirk in the makeup of the Hungarian peasants. As Domotor brings out, sordid material conditions, ruthless oppression by feudal lords and, later, by the unscrupulous representatives of early capitalism, pestilence, natural and man-made disasters, such as wars, the ubiquitous tax collectors—combined to make his existence here on earth so miserable that he needed a more immediate, concrete and dynamic champion to lean on than the Christian promise of succor in the afterlife.

While Hungarian peasant belief in the existence of witches, sorcerers, and in the táltos (priest-magician) existed up to the most recent times, there is little doubt that he did not take the stories he heard from the lips of the narrators as literal truth.

While recognizing the fairytale as fiction, he nonetheless held fast to the more tangible representations created by his primeval ancestors, including the pagan rites of shamanism, that had consoled the earlier Magyars in their migrations from somewhere in central Asia to their final settlements in what is now modern Hungary and the Alps of Transylvania, today a part of Western Rumania.

Before an examination of the nature of Hungary's specific contribution to the folk tale, a word on the status of folk beliefs in that country today. By the turn of this century the rural village had begun to shake itself loose from its thousand year dependence on its wizards and herbalists.

The huge strides in scientific education and modern agriculture, particularly after 1945, has relegated most of the old beliefs and fetishisms to the museum. Current researchers, unlike their colleagues of as recently as 25 years ago, can no longer choose any village at random to observe and photograph practices that in many respects were not that different from those around the year 1000. And, as we shall see, this change has had an enormous impact on the production of and receptivity to oral folk stories.

The Hungarian Folk Tale

General editor of *Folktales of the World*, Richard M. Dorson, states that no more than 5 percent of the 6,000 extant Hungarian folk narratives are available in other languages. Certainly those in English are far fewer than that.

Linda Dégh, who has edited a very commendable English translation of "Folktales of Hungary", published by the University of Chicago Press, states that the narrator of oral folk tales is still a popular figure in many areas of rural Hungary.

She, like other Hungarian ethnographers, ascribes the exceptionally rich texture of Hungarian oral literature to the prolonged exploitation of the peasant, who, as Domotor has pointed out, more than any other class in society had to bear a double burden: national oppression and the evils of feudalism. Even after the formal abolition of serfdom in 1848, the Hungarian peasant discovered, as did the Russian serf upon his "emancipation" in late 19th century Czarist Russia, that his lot, if anything, had become even more unbearable.

For the "freeing" of the Hungarian serf was accompanied by the infusion of bank capital into the huge manoral estates, driving the peasant off the land, to which he previously had been legally bound. Thus was created a rural proletariat of "three million beggars".

Just as the misery of the peasant poor insured the survival of the ancient magic practices rooted in pre-migratory history for almost a thousand years, so the same wretchedness provided the top soil for the flowering of the Hungarian oral folk tale as a welcome respite from social oppression and injustice.

Distinct types of Hungarian folk narratives number seven in all. The most popular by far—constituting more than half of the total corpus—is the Märchen or Fairytale. Others include such rubrics as Jokes and Anecdotes, Religious Tales, Animal Tales, Tales of Lying, Historic Legends, and Local Legends. Under this latter classification there are seven sub-headings including such items as Witches, Supernatural Beings, etc.

One of the unique features of most Hungarian folk tales is the wealth of detail incorporated into the typical story. While this is especially observable in the Fairytale, it is characteristic of the other genres as well.

Like a contrapuntal fugue of Bach there can be two, three, or more discrete plots and even sub-plots developing side by side in the tale. The greater the ingenuity of the storyteller the more complex and lengthy are his episodes and, in turn, his ability to connect them all up by story's end in a smooth, highly satisfying and logically consistent manner. This free-inventing technique has been so perfected by the individual narrators that few tales turn out to be mere variations of one another.

Yet, paradoxically, the raconteur is expected to conform quite rigidly to the genre's long-established structure, though within this framework he, as indicated, is permitted, indeed expected, to unfold his narrative with all the ingenuity at his command.

Closely associated with the required adherence to the generally accepted format of the Hungarian oral genre is the inclusion of certain fixed or stereotyped expressions of speech. For example, in the Fairytale "Handsome Andras", there is repeated reference, with only slight variations throughout, to the hero's positive trait of obedience: "Handsome Andras did as he was told" or "Well, Andras did as he was told".

Again in the Fairytale "Pretty Maid Ibronka" there are innumerable repetitions of the question by the girl's sweetheart as to what she saw looking through the keyhole. Invariably she answers "Nothing did I see looking through the keyhole" or "but nothing did I see looking through the keyhole."

In Hungarian such constant repetitions by the skilled narrator can produce a hypnotic atmosphere, inducing in the enraptured listener a euphoric state of mind.

True, that was precisely the function of storytelling, given the unrelieved toils and hazards of serfdom. Like a narcotic, it was able to transport the lowly peasant into the coveted land of magic, a feat which no biblical tale could duplicate.

Dégh has tape recordings of a talented Hungarian storyteller, an illiterate seventy-two-year-old night-watchman, who has 254 original stories in his repertory. There are a number of narrators who can start a tale one night and continue enlarging the same tale for weeks on end without repeating themselves and all the while keeping their listeners wholly absorbed.

Since 1945, due to a variety of causes such as widespread migration from the countryside to the industrial centers and easing of the burden of the peasant through land redistribution and scientific farming techniques, there has been a natural erosion of the art of storytelling.

However, opportunities for display of one's narrative

prowess are still possible in many villages of modern day Hungary despite the popularity of the cinema, of radio and television. Hostels frequented by itinerant workmen from a variety of trades, including herdsmen, farmhands, construction workers, and many others prefer the entertainment of skilled storytellers. These in turn welcome the chance to hone their craft before critical but highly appreciative live audiences.

But even in the villages a storyteller who can bring a little bit of theater, a bit of hamming into his act will not be wanting for invitations to appear at social events or at a gathering of the village folk performing certain common (and usually quite monotonous) laboring tasks.

By far the best way of ascertaining Hungary's unique contribution to the art of the folktale is to experience in person the dramatic interplay between the bard and his responsive listeners in those areas of the countryside where the art of storytelling still flourishes.

On the other hand if one's finances or the formidable language barrier requires a postponement of so delightful an adventure then the next best option is to read what has been published in translation.

In any case the reader will, I believe, discover for her- or himself, in the single specimen of this ingenuous Hungarian art form, recreated within each chapter in the book at hand, a bit of the wonder that a true and inspired word magician has been and is still able to evoke in his audience.

W. Z. Brust
St. Paul, Minnesota
October 1986